The Unexpected Third

L. Clara

Contents

Playlist

Middle Finger – ASTON

That's My Girl – Russ

Bruises – Lewis Capaldi

Glipse of Us – Conor Maynard

Burning Down – Alex Warren

Soulmate – Chanin

Loved Me Back to Life – Celine Dion

Rise Up – Smash Into Pieces

Still Worth Fighting For – My Darkest Days

Where You Go I Go – Fight The Fade

I'm sorry – Project Vela

Protector – City Wolf

Wildfire – Against The Current

Stay – Smash Into Pieces

Content / Trigger Warnings

Include but are not limited to

Homophobia

Polyamorous relationship

Parental neglect & rejection

LGBTQ relationships

Secret relationships

Mentioned SA (off page)

Mention of DV (off page)

Attempted murder

Involuntary Manslaughter

Sexually explicit language

Sexually explicit scenes

Note from the author

If you or anyone you know is struggling with their sexuality or need general support please call the General LGBT Hotline at 888-843-4564.

For additional LGBTQIA support lines please visit https://lgbthotline.org/

If you or anyone you know is a victim of domestic violence, please reach out for help.

National Domestic Violence Hotline 1-800-799-7233 Text "START" to 88788

If you or anyone you know is struggling with suicidal thoughts or going through a crisis, you can call or text the 988 Lifeline, which provides 24/7, free, and confidential support. Call or text them by dialing 988 or live message/chat with them at their website: https://988lifeline.org

If you or anyone you know is the victim of sexual assault please reach out to RAINN, the National Sexual Assault Telephone Hotline at 800.656.HOPE (4673)

You can also visit **online.rainn.org** to receive support via confidential online chat.

For the girls, gays, and theys, keep shining. Surround yourself with the people who make your light the brightest it can be.

Chapter One

Anya

My gaze meets my latest client, Mrs. Adams, in the mirror. Her fake n' bake spray tan looks obnoxiously fresh. She's giving Oompa Loompa circa 1971. I force my most professional smile as I apply the last bit of hair spray to her long golden locks. She asked for beach waves and yet, when I pick up my straightener and start to style the way she asks, she huffs out an annoyed breath.

"I'm so sorry, Mrs. Adams, did you change your mind on the beach waves?" My tone is much sweeter than it should be. From the moment this woman walked into our salon she's had a chip on her shoulder and has been combative about everything. If we weren't such a new salon I would have kicked her ass to the curb two bowls of bleach ago.

"How do you expect to curl my hair with a straightener? Do you even have a license to do hair?" The entitled attitude is going to get her thrown out of here if Axel hears how she's speaking to me.

"I'm sorry, Mrs. Adams. Not every stylist uses a curling iron for curls. Some of us prefer straighteners to curl." I smile softly before continuing. "If you'll allow me to show you what I can do with a straightener, I'm sure you'll like it."

After a moment of silence and then an annoyed grunt of agreement, I go through the steps of curling her hair with my tool of choice. With a resigned sigh she waves her hand and allows me to continue. Once it's done, she stands and gets close to the mirror, her critical gaze taking in her appearance.

"I will need to reschedule for four weeks." She snaps at me. No, she literally snaps her fingers at me like I'm a servant of some sort.

"Oh," I chuckle nervously. We're a new business, we must deal with Karens. No offense to the Karens that don't immediately have an attitude with the world around them. "Ok, we can schedule you for four weeks, ma'am."

Why did I ever get into an industry that makes me *"people"* all day? They're the worst. *Fucking hell.* I inwardly groan as Mrs. Adams follows me to the desk where I check my schedule. After her next appointment is on the books, she walks out with the same stick up her ass that she had when she walked in. Sometimes a fresh cut and color just isn't enough for every person who sits in my chair.

Not even five minutes after Karen, a party of one from the fires of hell, leaves does the front door open again. My shoulders slump for a moment in defeat. I need to pee, damnit! The greeting Axel and I painstakingly crafted over a box of wine and greasy cheese pizza is leaving my lips as I turn to face the newcomer.

"Hi! Welcome to Capelli Studio, do you have an appointment?" My feet are taking me toward the handsome man before I can stop myself, the need to empty my bladder temporarily forgotten. The stranger standing before me has at least a foot over my five foot six inches. His hair is covered by a dark baseball cap, but I'll see that soon enough. He's lean, but goddamn, is he muscular. The man looks like he could toss you around like it's nothing. *Holy fuck nuggets is this man sexy.*

"Hi, sorry, no. I just happened to have some free time, and I wanted to get my hair cut before my girlfriend gets home from lunch with her sister." Golden specks sparkle as the overhead lights shine into his eyes. Huh, kin to Edward and Carlisle? I smirk at the thought.

"That shouldn't be a problem, my name is Anya, I can take you back and get you done in a jiff. It doesn't look that bad from what I can see. Unless you're hiding more under that hat than meets the eye." I reply with a flirty wink. Shit, I shouldn't flirt with customers. I turn my back to him and motion for him to follow me to my station.

"Thanks! I'm Clay. I appreciate you taking me last minute like this." He smirks at me through the mirror as he takes a seat in my chair. My eyes roam down the length of his body. Damn, I can tell he's muscular just at how his shirt fits across his broad chest. I force myself to look back at his head. Right. Head, no – wait – hair, not head. Damnit, Anya. Focus!

I scrunch my nose with amusement when he pulls his cap off his head revealing a thick mop of dark blond waves that fall past his neck and hangs closer to his shoulders.

"Alright, maybe not a jiff." I giggle as I drape a cape around him.

I excuse myself for a quick bathroom break and to fan myself off. "Damn vagina, get it together. He has a girlfriend!" I quietly scold myself as I empty my bladder.

After I wash my hands and return to my station, Clay is sitting there with his eyes glued on me through the mirror. It's unnerving. I drag my fingers through his thick hair for a few minutes while we discuss length and style options. I move around to my styling station and open the drawer for my clippers. When I return to him, I see Clay's phone in his hand with an incoming call.

My heart beats erratically and ping pongs around the walls of my chest. *No, shit. Fuck. No, it can't be.* Her hair is different, now it's a bright teal, but those eyes, that smile. That face has been seared into my memory. I see her every time I close my eyes. If it weren't for the jar of Wickles Dirty Dill pickles in her hands in the picture, I could brush it off as a coincidence. Plenty of people are named Kat that have such unique Persian green eyes that you could get lost in for hours as you plan out your life together. Right? But the pickles on top of that. *Fuck. No. Fuck! She's not supposed to be here.*

Clay tilts the phone when he opens a text, and the privacy screen makes it so I can't see what he's saying. God damnit. I realize I haven't moved since the call came through when his golden-brown eyes find mine in the mirror and he speaks.

"Hey, are you ok?" He asks the question as if he's completely unaware. Maybe he is? "I'm sorry about that, my girlfriend called, and I figured it would be easier if I texted her instead."

I shake my head, a weak attempt to clear my mind. I feign a bright smile before replying.

"I'm great, I actually recognized your girlfriend, I haven't seen her since college, is all." My lips turn up into a forced smirk before I ask, "does she still hate the name Pickle?"

Clay snorts, "Oh my god, she threatens us any time we say it, one of her best girlfriends, Ryan, calls her Pickle constantly just to get a rise out of her."

He's oblivious to just how much this development has affected me. Granted, it's been so long since we've seen each other, he probably doesn't even know of my existence.

"So you and Kat were good friends?" He's sincere with his question.

"Yea, she was one of my best friends for a while and then life took us in different directions. I'm glad to hear she's doing well." I reply while I check the length of his hair on either side of his head to ensure everything is even.

"Why don't you come by for dinner tonight? I can have her grab pizza on her way home," Clay's excitement is palpable. *Fuck.* "I just need to talk to her about something, which is actually part of the reason I wanted to get my hair cut today. I think she'd love to see an old friend."

"Oh, I don't know, I don't want to intrude." I nearly choke on the words. Holy shit, this can't be real life right now. I squeeze a bit of hair gel into my hands before styling his hair.

He pushes me further, "come on, I won't take 'no' for an answer, she would love it."

"Um, alright." I force a smile as my insides twist into knots.

This is going to be a nightmare. Clay gives me his number and address before he leaves, I tell him I have another appointment, and I can come by in a while. I absolutely lied my ass off. I need to talk to Axel.

As soon as Clay is gone, I rush to the door and lock it behind him before I turn on my heel and run out the back to the small courtyard that connects our house with the salon. A light sheen of sweat coats my skin between the adrenaline and the anxiety of what just transpired.

I push the back door open, the wood slams into the plaster wall startling Axel who is in the kitchen shirtless. My breath comes out in pants as I try to form the words I need to explain the situation. Axel's glare bores into the side of my head.

"You little shit, you scared the hell out of me. What's going on?" His silky-smooth voice turns sour when he takes in what must be a chaotic expression.

"She lives here. Her boyfriend was just here." I choke out on a sob, "I told him I knew her when I saw her picture on his phone and he's insisting on having me over for dinner to see her tonight!"

"Oh damn, ok. Hold on." He turns off the audiobook I didn't realize was playing. What was that, Will Wheaton? This guy is listening to Ready Player One on repeat. He may be a nerd, but he's my nerd. Or I'm his pain in the ass, I'm not sure who claims who anymore.

"Axe, I can't, I can't do this!" My voice cracks as I speak, "I'm going to puke."

"Anya, listen to me." Axel's voice breaks through as he suddenly appears next to me, the warmth of his bare chest against my front as he holds me. "It's going to be ok. Why don't you go, get all done up and go see her. It's been years." He presses a kiss to my hair. "You've been a mess and torturing yourself since the day you left her. This could be the closure you've needed for years."

Silent tears fall down my cheeks as my best friend holds me together like he has since the day we met when I started cosmetology school after I left college. My body trembles as the anxiety becomes too much. Why does he have to be right, he's always right. Crap.

Axel holds me for a while until I find my strength. He follows me to my room to help me find an outfit when I finally make my decision, which let's be real - there was never a decision to make, we both know that the moment I saw her face that I would have moved heaven and earth for a way to see her again. The man is straight as an arrow, but he has an eye for hair and fashion, the latter I take advantage of to help my fashion-stunted ass. I'd walk around in a sports bra and yoga pants all day if I could get away with it.

After some arguing, we agree on a pair of tight jeans that make my ass look like I'm close personal friends with the Kardashian's surgeons and a flowy tank that has a plunging neckline. The girls may not be as big as Kat's, but they're decent. Fuck, I can't believe I'm about to see her again.

I pull on my Doc Martens, grab my keys from the front table and send Axel back to the salon to close everything up for the night. I can't concentrate on any of those tasks and he's been hoping for this reunion, no matter how unexpected it may be right now, for years. He's not going to argue with the reason why I made him work on his evening off.

Their place is only a few blocks away, but with the high likelihood of me needing a quick exit, I opt to drive over. It's a quick drive and I barely register the time between sliding the key into the ignition and when I arrive. *Shit.*

Once I push open my car door, I climb out and take a deep breath before pushing it closed and making my way to the entrance. It's seven p.m. so it's fairly dead outside of the gym. A petite, but cute woman that must be in her early twenties sits and has her head buried in a book when I enter. I smirk and turn in the direction that Clay mentioned when he told me where they lived. I find the office and walk up the stairs to find them spinning in a circle. Kat's beautiful teal hair is curled in loose waves and hangs down her back. Her body is even more defined than it was when I knew her in college. I'm not surprised, she was so dedicated to health and fitness with the career she wanted to pursue. I'd expect no less.

They're kissing and I hear a soft moan, I somehow find it in me to clear my throat before they go any further and this becomes even more painful to watch. Clay sets Kat on her feet and she turns to face me. Her eyes grow wide and her face pales. Shit, here goes.

"Hey, Anya!" Clay greets me, his arms still wrapped around Kat like it's the only way he can breathe.

"Hi, Pickle." I say the name I've been needing to for so long, tears prick at my eyes as I see the pain I'm causing her.

Yep, a nightmare.

Chapter Two

"Bunny." As the old pet name passes my lips, my stomach drops. A pain I haven't felt so strongly in years makes a sudden reappearance as my heart hammers against the walls of my chest. Chaos whirls around my mind as every thought, every painful memory that has haunted me for the past six years since she left, flashes before me all at once. My heart drops so hard, I swear I hear a sudden thud behind my ribcage.

This can't be real. Clay's muscular body goes rigid behind me, his strong arms tense and cage me against his chest. I choke back a sob as I force his arms away and give myself space to step away, not sure how I can trust the man I've called my best friend for six years. The thought feels ridiculous. Clay would never hurt me, but if that's true, why is she here?

"Clay," I whisper as I turn to face him, my gaze meets his. The confusion, rage, and pain clear on his face. "What is this?"

My soul feels like it's being broken into a million pieces all over again as I look into his eyes. I know he loves me; he would never intentionally hurt me. Why would he bring her here? What would make him think this was a good idea? Anya is the one that speaks from behind me.

"Pickle," Anya's voice breaks through the blood pounding in my ears as I try to make sense of everything. "He didn't know." Her voice is soft and gentle. Obviously, I'm not keeping my cool right now, but can you blame me?

My head whips around to face her, as angry and hurt as I feel, I can't deny she still looks fucking incredible. Her body has filled out nicely, her hips are full, and I can see with the skintight jeans she's wearing her thighs are thick and muscular. Her breasts are still perky, she chose a tank top that really shows off her assets and some stunning floral artwork tattooed on her left arm. It just pisses me off even more that I'm still so damn attracted to her.

Why did time have to be so damn good to her? Ugh!

"All I said to him was that you were my best friend." Anya's voice is soft and cautious. She tucks a long piece of hair behind her ear, I notice the pink at the ends, which makes my lips twitch into a quick smile as the memories of her love of the color come flooding back. I school my features before she has a chance to speak again. She can't know that she still has an effect on me after all this time.

Frustration builds as my blood boils through my veins as I start pacing the length of the living room. I don't understand why Anya would pull this. Why now? What does she have to gain from showing back up in my life like no time has passed? I groan as the anger bubbling in my chest needs a release from my body.

"Princess," Clay finally speaks, gently pulling my attention back to him. "Baby, I'm so sorry. I didn't know. You never said her name." I know he's right and I'm not mad at him. He was there through everything. The pain, the recovery, the hangover from hell. Fuck, there's no way he would do this to me on purpose, especially with where we are now.

When I glance back in Anya's direction, I notice her tender expression. And I snap. Before I can stop myself, I whirl around and rush toward her. My face is only inches from hers when I feel Clay's arms cage me against him once more to keep me from physically lashing out.

"No, Anya. *You* don't get to feel special right now. *He* was the one who picked up the pieces when I never heard from you again." I snarl at her, unable to hold back the venomous tone. "He is the one who helped heal what you broke. You don't get to feel happy when I haven't been able to even say your name for years. The only reason I was able to share anything with Clay is because I was so drunk the first time he met me, he had to carry me into the bathroom because I couldn't walk. That's the kind of shit show you left behind when you vanished out of my life."

Clay releases me when I'm done speaking, he must realize I needed to say my piece. Obviously, he would be the one to understand. He's been there since the day my relationship with Anya ended. He's the one who helped piece me back together when I could hardly function.

Anya takes a step back like she's been slapped. Good. She should feel like shit, this isn't about her. Okay, it is about her, but not in the way she's taking it.

Six years ago

My head hurts so badly, I can feel my pulse in my ears from the pain. I will never have another drink again. A pathetic moan passes my lips as I feel the couch dip next to me. Cautiously, I pry one eye open to see the beautiful man from earlier seated at my feet.

"What do you want?" I whimper as I roll onto my side to grab the bucket he left for me in case I vomit again. At this point, it's just dry heaving as there is nothing left in my stomach.

"Since I'm not sure what your poison is for a hangover cure, I came back with some options." He announces with pride as he hands over a blue Gatorade. "I brought some of the greasiest burgers and fries I could find and Taco Bell. My old roommate swore by a full English breakfast so I got the closest thing I could find from the diner a few blocks down. And your fresh toast will be done soon." His beautiful smile is infectious and perfectly timed with the pop of the toaster. He chuckles as soon as he hears the pop, obviously amused by his impeccable timing.

"Ugh, I hate you. But I'll take the tacos and the fries." I groan again as I hold my hands out in front of me for the food and making gimme motions. "You know what, just leave it all."

He chuckles, obviously amused by my pain, but he hands over the goods. Several hours later, I've finished most of the food and feel somewhat more human. I realize when I finally sit up from where I've been camped out all day on the couch, I don't remember if this beautiful stranger has even given me his name.

"Who are you again?" The question passes my lips just before I take the last bit of taco into my mouth. I moan around the delicious greasy flavors.

"Clay, I just moved in down the hall a few weeks ago." He replies with a smile. His demeanor is calm, and he doesn't appear to be annoyed. So, hopefully I haven't asked him before. "Becca and I had run into each other a few times since I moved in, and apparently, she doesn't spend enough time around the building to know anyone else to ask for help when she had to leave this morning." He shrugs.

"Well, thank you for your service." With a heavy sigh I climb to my feet. "I won't keep you any longer. I'm sorry you felt like you had to stay with me all –" I check the time on my phone. "Holy shit, you've been here all day! I'm so sorry!" I groan and flop back down onto the couch with an audible sigh. "Not only am I a freaking mess, but I took your entire day from you."

"You didn't take anything away from me. I'm happy to be here. Plus, I've been able to re-watch Jersey Shore." His laugh is low and wicked. Fuck, why does he have to be attractive? "Granted, I haven't been able to figure out how to get out of the streaming service your TV is set to so that was the best option I've had."

"So, you're telling me that you've been watching a bunch of twenty somethings get trashed all day while you've taken care of my hungover ass?" I stare at this beautiful man in awe. Why is he so nice? No one has ever been this kind to me.

"Yep, and in case you were wondering, you have a cute snore." Clay winks at me before he turns back to the TV and picks up the remote and presses the button to pause the show. "Go shower, I'll clean up your smorgasbord."

A shy smile dances across my lips as I stand to my feet again and slowly walk to the bathroom. My mind is a wonderland of sadness, pain, and gratitude. The latter is obviously for Clay. I hope we can become friends so that I can somehow repay him for such kindness.

gratitude. The latter is obviously for Clay. I hope we can become friends so that I can somehow repay him for such kindness.

Chapter Three

Anger rolls off Kat in waves as she shoots daggers at Anya with her eyes. *Fuck.* She is going to lose herself again in this and it's my fucking fault. God damnit. I should have put two and two together. I'm so fucking dense.

The moment she said "Bunny," I knew. Granted, I never knew her given name, but it had always hurt Kat too badly, she had never mentioned a real name. Just that fucking pet name. Fuck, I have hated her from the moment I saw Kat laying on the bathroom floor all those years ago and now to see her in person. I hate her even more that I wanted to share her with Kat. What the fuck is wrong with me?

"Princess," I speak up, interrupting their argument or conversation. I'm not exactly sure what's happening. When Kat looks back to me, I continue my explanation. "Baby, I'm so sorry. I didn't know. You never said her name."

Kat turns back to Anya and lays into her when she recognizes Anya was feeling important because I knew about her existence. When she finally finishes saying her piece, she leans back into me. My heart breaks for my girl when I feel her knees give out from under her. The exhaustion of the confrontation steals her ability to stand on her own two feet. Slowly, I lower her to the seat of the closest chair. Anya's eyes look sad, she can see what she's causing right now, yet she's still here.

"I'm sorry, Kat. I just." Anya lets out a pained breath, "I needed to see you again."

I stand to escort Anya out, but she takes a card out of her purse and lays it on the coffee table before backing away slowly.

"I'm leaving, but if you decide you want to talk. Call or text me, day or night." She turns to leave, but pauses when she gets to the door. "You look good, Pic. Take care of her, Clay."

Kat's shoulders begin to shake as sobs shudder through her. I walk over to the door that leads to my office and lock it before I return to the couch and hold my girl close to me. I give her the space she needs to let out all the feelings that just came back up.

"I'm so sorry, baby, so sorry." I repeat as I press my lips to her hair in a soft kiss.

My thoughts are torn between making sure she's ok and selfishly worried she's going to leave me over this. God damnit, I just got her. I can't lose her. Kat must sense my anger because she pulls back to look at me, tears falling down her cheeks.

"Clay," her soft voice comes out as more of a whimper.

"Yea, Princess?" I ask quietly.

"I love you, I'm sorry I never told you her name. This is my fault." She sobs and buries her face in my chest.

"No Babygirl," I wrap my arms around her even tighter in hopes it brings her some sort of calm. "It's a fucked-up situation but it's not your fault. You were in pain losing her the way you did. She should have been more honest when I insisted she come over. I just thought it would be good for you to see an old friend."

We sit there like that for several minutes before I speak again.

"Though, I guess I should have known when she was hesitant to accept." I sigh into the quiet room. The only sound is Kat's gentle sobs.

After a while Kat's breathing has steadied signaling that she's fallen asleep in my arms. I smirk remembering the first time this happened, and lift her from the couch to carry her back to our bed.

Once she's settled in bed, I return to the living room and grab my phone. I dial the only number that I know she'd want to talk to about this. We've never actually spoken, but I've had his number for a while in case of emergency situations. What a great way to introduce myself, *'Hey, I'm in love with your sister, but I just broke her heart by accidently bringing her ex-girlfriend home the same day I asked her to move in with me.'*

"Hello?" A deep voice answers the phone.

"Hey, Augustus?" I pause, but when no acknowledgment that I have the correct number comes I continue, "This is Clay. Kat's boyfriend."

"What happened?" His voice has become less cautious and more concerned with whatever is going on with his sister.

"Anya is in town, and I may have invited her over not realizing it was her..." I let the implication die on my tongue. The line goes dead for a few minutes, I pull the phone away from my ear to make sure it hasn't disconnected. "Hello?"

"I'm here, dumbass. Where is Kat?" He asks with an amused tone to his voice.

"She's in bed right now, but I know you're the only person she'd feel comfortable talking to about everything, given her friend's are currently otherwise occupied." I admit. "I may have been there the first time around, but now that she and I are dating, I worry she may not want to confide in me. I don't want her to be alone."

"I'll keep my phone on me. Don't underestimate her feelings for you, though." He chuckles, "She's been smitten by you for much longer than she's willing to admit."

The call disconnects and I stand there with so much more confusion than when I first made the call. I need to have this conversation with Kat. My heart is in my throat as I head back to our room and tug my T-shirt over my head. After folding it, I place the piece of clothing on the top of the dresser followed by my jeans.

Kat is tucked into the fetal position on the bed, just like she was when I left. My heart breaks all over again as I take in the sight. This beautiful, intelligent, and incredible woman being brought to her knees by someone who trampled on her heart once before only infuriates me to my core.

As I watch her sleep, I realize, I'll never stand in her way if she wants to have Anya in her life. But I'll be damn sure to make Anya know exactly what she's done to my girl and the trauma she's taken so long to heal from. I cross the room to the bed, lifting the covers to slide in behind Kat. Once I'm settled, I pull her sleeping form closer to me and bury my face in the crook of her neck. It only takes moments before I finally succumb to the events of the day and my own exhaustion pulls me under.

Chapter Four

Anya

Six years ago

 I've been sitting on my bed for the last hour chatting on the phone with my mom. I smile into the phone as we reminisce about my time in cheer, rah, rah, sis, boom, bah or something like that. That is until she brings up a topic I'm so not prepared for.

"That girl you were friends with," there's a momentary pause as she remembers the name she's looking for. "Jamie, from high school?" My mother mentioning my first girlfriend's name makes my heart stop. She doesn't know about my sexual identity. I haven't found the courage to tell her. I have no idea how my dad would handle me coming out. Shit.

"What about her?" The question comes out a little harsher than I mean for it to.

"She's, you know..." the pause that passes before she says what I already know, is torturous. "She's gay!" my mother whisper-shouts into the phone like it's the plague.

"Ok, and?" I respond cautiously as I drag my knees up to my chest.

"I could never!" She doesn't bother hiding her disgust. "She came out to her parents last week and she's been flaunting her new girlfriend around town!"

"If she's happy, why does it matter?" I ask as tears begin to prick at my eyes.

"She's not going to be happy ten years from now when she can't have children!" Mom scoffs into the phone.

"Mom, don't you think that's kind of backwards? I mean, it's her life." My mind goes into damage control in an attempt to get ahead of the inevitable situation.

"It can be her life without her telling the world! Sweetpea, I'm so thankful that you aren't like....that." She scoffs yet again as she whispers the last word. "I wouldn't be able to look at you as my child anymore."

"You would disown me if I fell in love with a woman?" My voice shakes, unable to hide my shock.

"Of course we would! That's just not how people are supposed to live!" She continues on a rant about what so-called 'real couples' are for another

twenty minutes before I find the courage to tell her I have to hang up for a study group.

Tears flow freely from my eyes as I replay the conversation with my own mother in my head. I can't afford to survive without them. They're paying for school and my housing too. Fuck! I can't lose my family. I've seen what it's done to Kat. Shit!

My body trembles as sobs wreck through me. Unable to sit still any longer I slide to the edge of the bed and stand. My emotions are overwhelming as I think through every scenario if I stay with Kat, my Pickle. If I stay here. I'm already so in love with her, staying will mean losing my family. Fuck!

I need to see her, to explain. Tears continue to fall as I walk the short distance to her dorm to explain what's happening. The moment I see her face though, my heart shatters yet again and it takes me a while to speak.

Kat dropped me off in my dorm room a week ago. I only lasted an hour before I called my mom, the tears as strong as they were when she and I first spoke. A made-up story about being home sick and needing to be back with my mommy and daddy, and now that's exactly where I am. In my childhood bedroom staring at the same four walls that I used to when I was a kid.

Nothing about this is fair, I miss Kat like I would miss air. She's in my every thought and every dream but I know if I stayed at school, it would have been worse. I would have gone back to her, and I would have lost my family.

"Anya! Sweetpea! It's getting late, don't you start classes today?" I hear my dad's voice as he hollers from the bottom of the stairs.

"Coming, Daddy!" I shout back.

Yep, this is my life now. I am going to cosmetology school so that I can earn my room and board. I mean, I guess it's fair. I wouldn't want to just sit around and do nothing all day. A frustrated groan passes through my lips as I check my hair and make-up in the mirror. It feels weird, being all dolled up like this, that was usually something Kat loved, but if I'm going to be working in the beauty industry, it seems like I'd need to take more time with my appearance.

After several minutes of contemplation, I decided on my all black romper. Not only does it accentuate what little curves I do have nicely, but it also has an opening in the crotch so I don't have to fully undress to pee. Listen, it's the little things when you're heartbroken.

My drive to the Oak Brook Cosmetology School is an easy forty-minute drive. Since this is one of the top schools in the country and it's so close, it seemed like a smart choice to apply. Never in my wildest dreams did I expect them to have a last-minute opening for the classes starting this semester. As soon as I park in front of the large modern building, I let out a sigh. Here goes nothing.

My first few days at Oak Brook were uneventful. Okay, not exactly uneventful. The moment I walked in I met a guy, Axel. He's super sweet and has taken me under his wing. I'm not sure why, but he has been insistent on keeping me close.

"Hey, An!" Axel shouts as soon as I walk into the classroom. Without a real moment to grasp what's happening, the man is rushing toward me with a giant smile on his face. "Here's some java to help with whatever is happening on your face." His teasing tone takes me by surprise as he hands me a fresh cup of coffee.

"I don't even know how to respond to that bit about my face, but thanks for the coffee," my response is laced with sarcasm. As soon as I take my first sip of caffeine, we both get lost in a fit of laughter.

"Ahh, kid. This is the beginning of a beautiful friendship." The sincerity in his tone and the grin on his face breathes a little light back into me as he wraps an arm around my shoulder while he pulls me toward the station he saved next to his.

"Did you really just Bogie me?" I step back with feign horror in my voice.

"Seems like I did, and you didn't say I'm wrong so shut up." He continues his onslaught of teasing.

"Okay, but I'm not leaving Casablanca any time soon there, Rick." Axel snorts at my response before getting himself situated at his station.

Two years later

Axel and I have been working together at a local salon for the last three months. We both graduated from Oak Brook tied for top of the class. We constantly compete and work to better our techniques. Our plan is to buy a place and open a salon together in a few years. Right now, I'm still just trying to get through the days without thinking about Pickle. You'd think after two years it wouldn't be so hard and yet, here we are. It's a Friday night, and I'm cuddled up in my bed watching old episodes of Friends and wishing I could be free to be myself. A frustrated groan escapes when I hear my text tone ding from across the room. Knowing if I ignore him he'll just keep bothering me, I stand and walk to grab the phone. When I press the side button to illuminate the screen, I roll my eyes before I type out a response.

Rick:

Louis! Let's go out, my treat. We can even go to that club outside of town, so you don't have to limit yourself.

Anya:

I really regret telling you about her. I just want to stay home. One of us has to save money for our eventual studio.

Rick:

That's a lie. You would be even more of a disaster if you didn't have me to confide in. Come on, maybe some Axe wound will do you good!

Anya:

What the fuck is an Axe wound?

Rick:

You know, pussy. Obviously. I dick them down so good their pussy is sore.

Anya:

Oh my god, okay, I'll come but promise to never call a vagina an Axe Box again or I will cockblock you any chance I get. How do you even get the women you do? Jesus!

Rick:

It's just part of my charm, now let's go! I'm outside, don't make me come to your door and ask your daddy if you can come out to play.

Anya:

I hate you.

Rick:

Love you too, boo bear.

After a quick wardrobe change and a light layer of makeup, I race downstairs to find that Axel is already on my couch and talking to my dad. I glare daggers at him which only makes him chuckle. He stands to greet me, wrapping his arms around me in a tight hug.

"Hey, Louis, let's blow this popsicle stand." His infectious grin has me smiling in a matter of seconds. God, he can be infuriating.

"Ugh, let's go, Rick." I roll my eyes at him as we head outside into the cool evening air and make our way to his car. "Seriously, Ax, I thought you were going to wait for me out here."

"I was, but I got bored and your dad likes me." He shrugs like that's a sufficient enough reason.

The night goes by far too fast; I've been wrapped up in a leggy brunette for the past few hours. When they signal for last call, I drag her over to the bar with me to pay my and Axel's tab because of course he's disappeared with some chesty redhead. What can I say, the man has a type.

"Do you want to grab a bite, then we can go back to my place?" Leggy brunette asks with a lust filled gaze.

I press a soft kiss against the sensitive spot just behind her ear and whisper a response that leads us to the closest gas station that sells alcohol. We're standing in line with a bottle of vodka in one hand while my hand is wrapped around Leggy's neck as I kiss the fuck out of her. A throat clears from behind us urging us forward. When I pull away, I see my parents, my mom's eyes wide as she takes in the scene before them.

Fuck. Me.

Chapter Five

I 'm still laying in the same position I was when I cried myself to sleep last night. I know at one point Clay got in bed with me. The feel of his arms wrapped snugly around me as he tucked me close to him and held me throughout the night is what allowed me to sleep so long. But now that my eyes flutter open as the rays of sunlight force me into the land of the living, I feel a coolness at my back that wouldn't be there if he were still in bed with me. I groan and pull the comforter over my head. Did last night really happen?

"Kat?" I hear his deep smooth voice call from not too far away.

My imagination has been running rampant since the moment I saw her. I curse under my breath and proceed to ignore his request for my attention or confirmation that I'm awake. My heart just isn't ready for this conversation.

"Baby, I know you're up. And I have coffee." He announces from somewhere in the room. "Please, Kat." The crack in his voice is what forces me to show my face.

Slowly, I lower the blanket to see Clay leaning against the door frame, his beautiful broad chest is bare and on display while his lower half is only covered by a thin pair of grey sweats. He looks like he barely slept last night. He takes a step toward me, apprehension clear in every move he makes. He places the mug of coffee on the bedside table before he falls to his knees next to the bed where I'm still laying.

"Clay, I love you, but to quote the genius that is David Rose, *I'm trying very hard not to connect with people right now.*" My eyes implore him to give me a little more time to digest what has happened.

He shakes his head, and I see a determination in his eyes that tells me he isn't going to let me hide. Sometimes I hate that he knows me so freaking well.

"Kat, I know you. If we don't talk right now, you're going to shut down on me." He lets out a heavy sigh. "I swear to you, I did not know."

Tears begin to fill my eyes again. I've cried so much in the last twelve hours you'd think I'd be used to it. Nope, not even a little.

"Princess, I love you. So goddamn much." Clay lets out a long breath as he leans his forehead against my side on the bed. "I wouldn't do anything like this to hurt you. Not after I saw the hell you went through when she left. I just want you to be happy." He admits on a shaky breath.

"*You* make me happy." Tears threaten to fall as I speak, "I know you didn't mean for any of this to happen. I don't blame you and I'm so sorry that I made you feel like I was." Frustration builds as I continue to speak my love for him, but resentment for her mixes in with my words. "Clay, I'm just feeling so many emotions that I can't put words to. I can't believe she would show up here like it wouldn't cause me pain. She made her choice all of those years ago. Why now? None of it makes any sense!" I sob.

He climbs in the bed in front of me and holds me close to his warm muscular body. A mix of sobs and whimpers are the only sounds I'm capable of as the memory of Anya being here rushes through me again.

"Princess, I know I make you happy, and not only in the dirty way." He winks at me with a sly smirk dancing across his lips which makes me giggle.

"Ughh! Clay!" I groan through a laugh.

"Do you want to talk to her? To see what she has to say about all of this?" He asks gently as he tightens his hold around me, like he's afraid I'll run from him or from us.

"I – I don't know." I admit. My heart beats a staccato rhythm as I allow the question to marinade. Could I handle talking to her? What could she say to make any of my pain better?

"Kat, be honest with me. I saw the way you looked at her. How your body reacted to her proximity." Fuck, this hurts so badly.

"I love you; we are all that I care about." I whisper through the pain in my chest as I motion to myself and then him.

"Don't. It's ok, you don't have to sugar coat it. I think if you say it out loud, it may help you heal, baby." Once I feel his arms wrap tightly around me the pain and tears crash into me yet again. He doesn't say anything else, just allowing me to internally digest my feelings while he further proves that he isn't going anywhere.

"I – I'm so fu – fucking scared," my confession is muffled by my face buried in his chest.

"I know, baby." Clay's simple response is enough to make my heart shatter all over again.

"What do I do?" The question passes my lips before I can stop myself.

"Oh, beautiful. Only you can make that decision." He chuckles darkly. "As much as I want to keep you for myself for the rest of our lives, I'm not going to stop you from however you want to have this play out." He gently grips my chin, tilting my face to look into his eyes. "But baby, even if you decide to allow her in again, in your life or in our bed, nothing on this earth will take me away from you. You're mine." The way his voice becomes a growl sends heat pooling between my legs.

"Yours" I agree with a panting whisper as my mouth finds his. "Clay," I whimper against his lips.

His answering growl is all I need to give in to my desperate desire for him. He groans into the kiss as my fingers find the waistband of his pants and tug them down his waist. My breath hitches as his hand grips the nape of my neck and he flips me onto my back without breaking the kiss. Clay pulls away briefly to shuck off the pants, freeing his rock-hard cock. The feeling of his length against my belly as he settles back between my legs has me whimpering yet again.

"I need you," I cry out as I try to find the friction my body is so desperately yearning for.

"Fuck, Kat." He growls against my neck as I push him onto his back once again. My fingers grip the bottom of my shirt, and I drag it over my head to expose myself. Once my breasts are on display, Clay sits up to pull a nipple into his mouth. I cry out at the delicious onslaught on my sensitive peaks. My hips begin to grind against him, his hard length finding the friction I've been so needy for.

"Oh God, Clay." I whine as the pleasure builds in my core. He grins at me with a dark chuckle before I hear a loud tear of fabric, I look down just in time for him to tear the side of my thong that is still connected. He pulls it away from my body and tosses it somewhere on the floor.

"Take my cock in that tight little pussy and take what you need, Princess." His smile is wicked as he props his hands under his head as he watches me.

"Fuck!" My words come out as a whimper. I rise up to give us just enough room to grant us what we both want. Unable to find patience, once I feel the crown of his cock at my entrance, I slam my ass down against his hips. "Claayy!" His name comes out somewhere between a moan and a whine as I take him all in one quick motion.

"God damn, Kat." He groans, his hands quickly move to my hips and hold me still for a moment while he adjusts to the sudden feel of me. "You're going to be the fucking death of me, Babygirl." I giggle at his reaction. "Fuck! I can feel your laugh in your cunt."

Instead of speaking, once his grip on my ass loosens, I rise back up and slowly guide myself back down onto his cock. His cock fills me in a way I've never experienced and this angle has me ready to scream with the ecstasy his body provides. I can see the restraint in Clay's face as he digs his nails into my hips again. He's trying so hard not to blow which just makes me want to earn his release even more. I grind my hips in a circle each time I am fully seated, my pussy clenching tighter around him each time. It's easy to tell the moment he gives up his determination. His eyes are dark with a heated gaze as he thrusts up from underneath me. My cunt convulses at the sensation.

"Fuck me, Clay! I'm going to –" The words die on my lips as I reach the peak of my pleasure.

I've been awake for a few hours. Clay showered and has gone down to work; this man is the definition of perfection. Covering for me at work while I have a mental breakdown. Granted, he's technically my boss so it's not like he'd fire me, but still. He's not pushing me.

A frustrated noise, somewhere between a groan and a growl, rumbles free as I grab my phone.

Kat:

An, I don't know what to say to you, but I know we need to talk. When are you free?

Chapter Six

Anya

The incessant siren that is my morning alarm forces me out of dream land. Sleep evaded me for most of the night, so today is going to be oh, so fun! I grab my phone from my bedside table and silence the annoying tone. Unfortunately, for anyone within a three-mile radius, I need the loudest alarm ever to actually function in the mornings. They're not my favorite part of the day. It's why I avoid opening at all costs, but Axe had an appointment this morning so I have to step up. I curse under my breath as I sit up and hang my legs over the side of the bed.

The sun has barely risen and I'm already up. I need coffee, fuck, do I need coffee. Once my feet lower to the ground I scrunch my toes in the shag area rug. The feeling makes me giggle without fail. As soon as I rise to my feet, I stretch my arms over my head and wake up my muscles so they're ready for whatever is going to happen today. With a frustrated groan I walk out of my bedroom and head down the hallway toward the bathroom. My morning routine has been the same every single day since I was a kid.

My mouth is minty clean now as I leave the bathroom and head toward the stairs. My body hasn't quite woken up yet, so I grip the railing as I take the steps down to the main living space. Realizing I left my phone by my bed when I reach the last step, I shrug knowing the only person that would be reaching out to me at this hour lives with me. I'll get it when I get dressed.

"Good morning, Louis!" Axel's chipper voice startles me, opening the back door wearing the same thing he had on last night as I stroll into the kitchen. "How was last night?"

"Let's just say we may need to close up shop and find another town before we really get started." I groan, my feet take me toward the coffee pot that was thankfully set up to brew twenty minutes ago. I pull out two mugs from the cabinet above and fill both as I continue. "He really had no clue it was me. She broke down when she saw me."

"Damn, I was hoping for better news." He crosses the distance and wraps me in a hug. "We're not closing the shop though. Get that thought out of your mind, she'll either come around or you will find someone even better. I can feel it in my bones."

I rest my head against his shoulder and let out a shaky breath. "Thank you, Rick." He lets me stand there for a few minutes to process a little of the past twenty-four hours before he forces me to function again.

"Go get dressed and open the shop, I need to shower and head out for my appointment." He lets out an exaggerated yawn.

I roll my eyes and yawn back at him. He chuckles at me as I grab my coffee and rush back upstairs. The java kicks in in record time which allows me to get dressed and to the shop in just under twenty minutes; granted it's only in our back yard, or we're in its back yard, or maybe it's that we share a backyard. We haven't really figured out how to explain that one.

I have the doors unlocked and ready for our first clients just as one of our stylists, Lori, walks in. Her silky golden locks are pulled up into space buns. A wide grin spreads across her face when she sees me.

"Hey, An!" She's so bubbly way too early in the morning. I hate her. "I know you don't like mornings; so, I brought you a peace offering." She skips, yes, the girl is so goddamn chipper, she skips towards me. A large cup of coffee in her outstretched hand as she approaches me. Ok, I changed my mind. I love her.

"You are the most beautiful thing I've seen in my life." I squeal as I take the cup from her. My lips wrap around the opening of the lid, and I take a generous sip. As soon as the delicious liquid slides onto my tongue, I whimper. My eyes go wide once I swallow. Holy shit, that's good. I take notice of the Mud House logo on the side; I'll absolutely be going there.

"Why do you never talk to me like that?" Lori's laugh is contagious as she turns away from me to prep her station.

"Sorry sweets, coffee is the love of my life." I swallow hard as the words pass my lips. Images of Kat's heartbroken expression haunt me. Well, it's one of the loves of my life. It takes several attempts to regain my composure before I can get my mind back into the number of clients I know are scheduled for today.

Our morning goes by in a flurry as clients come in with appointments and as walk-ins. My mind is thankful for the distraction from the painful thoughts, but my body is ready for a nap. By the time the morning rush slows and Axe shows up for his shift, we have a chance to breathe so I pull out my phone. A gasp escapes as I see the notification on the screen. My hands begin to tremble as I read and carefully type out a reply.

Kat:

> An, I don't know what to say to you, but I know we need to talk. When are you free?

Anya:

> Kat. There is so much I need to say. I'm at work right now but Axe is closing so I'll have the house to myself. Do you want to come to my place at 3:30?

She must have had her phone in her hand because the response is quick.

Kat:

> Who's Axe? You know what, never mind. It's not my business. I'll see you then.

Is she jealous? There's no way. As I tell myself not to think further into her messages, I can't help the smile that stretches across my face. Maybe all hope isn't lost.

"What's with your face?" Axel's voice pulls me from my thoughts. I feel his gaze boring into the side of my face before I turn to him.

"She texted me; she's coming over when I leave here." I reply quietly, afraid to speak any louder with how big this is.

"Shut your whore mouth! Why are you still here? Go get all dolled up, bitch!" His excitement is startling. Lori and I both stare at him after his outburst for a minute before I respond.

"Uh, I have an appointment coming in five minutes." I roll my eyes at him.

"I don't care if the Grandson of Sam walks in that door, I will take the bullet for you. Get the fuck out of here." He's vibrating with excitement as he speaks.

What the fuck. "You're saying you'll sacrifice yourself to a potential murderer just so I have time to get changed before she gets here?"

"Fuck, yes!" He chuckles.

"Uh, I'm not taking that bullet," Lori chimes in, her voice cracks. She's not one for true crime conversations.

Axe and I stare at each other and erupt with laughter realizing she took him seriously. I shake my head.

"He's being dramatic. No one is going to come in here to shoot you. You're fine, sweets." I snort. "Alright, fine. If you're so good, you can work two appointments at once." My lips twitch at the challenge knowing he won't be able to say no.

After going through every piece of clothing I have in my closet and dresser, my room is trashed with clothing strewn everywhere. I'm wearing a dark gray crop top that cuts off low enough to hide the *naughty bits* but high enough that the smooth skin of the underside of my breasts are peaking out. My torso is on full display, my ass is barely covered in a pair of black booty shorts that have a picture of my namesake on the hip dressed in the god awful easter bunny costume.

The past ten minutes have been spent pacing back and forth in the living room as I wait for her to arrive. Finally, a soft knock sounds against the front door. I muster up all the calm I possibly can and open the door to see Kat standing there in a Pop Evil T-shirt tied at her back and a pair of yoga pants. Her eyes are red and puffy with dark circles like she's not stopped crying since I left. Immediately, I feel like even more of an asshole.

"Pic, come in." I move aside to let her walk past me.

"Don't, please." She whispers as she steps into my space.

Unable to help my smile when I get a whiff of her shampoo. "You still have a love for cherry blossoms?"

"They're my favorite," she shrugs.

We stand there staring at one another for what could be seconds, minutes, or hours just taking each other in. She breaks the silence after I'm not sure how long.

"Anya, I need to know what happened. You just vanished." She whispers. "Now, you suddenly appear in my town, with my boyfriend of all people."

Her eyes are pleading. I take a deep breath and motion for her to take a seat on the couch so I can explain.

Chapter Seven

Anya

Time has been so good to her; I can't help but take her in as Kat sits next to me. Her teal hair is up off her neck in a messy bun. Even though she looks as exhausted and emotional as I feel, there is no one else in this world that could hold a candle to her beauty. I hold off for as long as I can to explain everything that happened when I left like I did, offering a drink and a snack before she snaps at me.

"Anya, just talk to me. You owe me that." The anger in her voice and pain I see in her eyes breaks my heart all over again.

"Ok. Well, before I came to you that day I had talked to my mom, and she had some really awful and ugly things to say when she found out that my ex-girlfriend had come out and was flaunting it." I begin and she growls at me.

"I fucking know all this." Damn, she's not going to make this easy. "Stop stalling, Anya. What the fuck happened?"

"What you don't know is that as soon as you took me back to my dorm, I broke down even more than I had when we had talked. I knew that I wouldn't be able to stay away from you if I stayed there." I pause and stare at her until her eyes find mine. "Kat, I've never loved anyone like I love you and the thought that I would have lost my family and their help with school if I stayed, I didn't want to put you in that position. I called my mom and made up some shit about being home sick."

I spend the next hour explaining what happened in those first two years between cosmetology school and meeting Axe. The expression on her face softens when she realizes I haven't seriously dated anyone since I left her. That is, until I tell her about the leggy brunette that I still can't for the life of me remember her name. Jealousy radiates off her in waves as I continue. It shouldn't be cute, but I'm not gonna lie, it makes me happy to know she has some kind of reaction. When I realized that she was the girlfriend Clay was talking about, I got jealous. Though I'm not sure if I'm jealous of her or him. Maybe both, they are both fucking stunning.

"When they saw us, my mom looked like she had been stabbed in the chest. My dad had no reaction that I could see." I swallow hard, allowing myself a minute before I tell her the part that's going to piss her off. "The thing is, they weren't mad. My dad was just happy to see me living my life and not hiding away in my bedroom. My mom had more questions than anything, but she wasn't mad. I told them about you. Why I came home from college and why everything changed so quickly."

Tears roll down her cheeks as I speak, I lean forward and wipe away the drops with my thumb. She presses her cheek against my palm which makes my breath catch. Kat must realize what she did because her face is suddenly no longer in my hand. I drop my arm back down and twist my fingers in my lap before continuing my story.

"The thing is when they found out I was ready to run again. I expected it to be a dream and when I woke up the next morning all of my stuff would be packed, and they'd throw me out. When that wasn't what happened, I broke down all over again. After Jamie had come out, her family had really rallied behind her. They cut off anyone who was even the teensiest bit rude or judgemental toward her. Apparently it helped my parents have a change of heart." I try to meet her gaze again, but she refuses to look at me.

"Did you stay with her that night?" Kat's question comes out as a whisper.

"What? Who?" I ask, confused by the query.

"The girl that they caught you with."

I choke back a laugh at the ridiculousness of her thought process.

"No baby, I didn't." My response is gentle before I add, "Any interest I had at that point dried up when I had to face my parents."

"An," tears are still streaming down her face, but she won't look at me. I keep my hands in my lap, afraid to upset her if I try to wipe her cheeks again. "Why didn't you come back for me?"

I let out a defeated sigh. There it is. The question I've been dreading.

"I was afraid. Afraid you had moved on, that you hadn't moved on. I was fucking terrified that you would react the way you did last night, and I'd break your heart like I knew I had back then." My confession gets stuck in my throat for a minute before I finally find my words again. "I was afraid that you'd hate me for leaving you and the reason I left ended up not being the reality when they found out. As more time has passed, I've just kept in my mind that you were off living out your happily ever after with someone who deserves you. Which in fairness, it looks like you are with your person."

"Wow." She shakes her head, "I don't even know how to respond to that." She chuckles darkly.

"I didn't push to come back with Clay last night. If anything, I tried to avoid it. But your boyfriend is persistent as hell." My voice comes out harsher than I mean it to.

Her laughter echoes around the room. "I know. He told me this morning." She admits.

"Then when I saw you, my god. Everything, every memory, feeling, desire, it all came rushing back and took the air from my lungs." A tear falls from my eye as I admit the scariest part of all of this.

"Listen, Anya. I don't –" she doesn't get to finish when I interrupt.

"I need you to know." My words are rushed. "I didn't come here for you, had I known you were still here, I would have made Axe choose a different town."

Kat nods in response. "I don't know what to say."

We sit in silence for a while before I finally look back up and find her eyes locked on me. Her lips part as she takes a deep breath. My tongue darts out wetting my lips and I see her swallow hard, her eyes following my every move when I do. She's still just as affected by me as I am by her.

Thoughts escape me as my body moves on its own accord. I close the distance between us, my lips press against her soft pout. Her breath hitches, she stiffens for a half a second until my tongue swipes against her lips and her body melts into mine as she opens to me, allowing access.

I moan as her sweetness explodes on my taste buds. My hands find the nape of her neck, my fingers dive into her hair, and I hold her where I want her as I devour her in a kiss that I've dreamed of for so long.

Suddenly, she pulls away. We stare at one another panting for breath when she speaks, "I – I can't do this." She stands up and rushes to the door. "This was a mistake. I shouldn't have come here. I can't do this to Clay." The wood slams against the frame as she runs out, shoving it closed once she's outside.

Before I can make a move or respond she's gone. Fuck. I flop back down onto the couch and groan.

"God damnit!" I whine as the back door swings open.

"Honey I'm ho –" Axel doesn't finish his thought when enters the living room and sees my expression. "Shit, what happened."

We sit on the couch, and I bare my heart to him reliving the last two hours of my life with Kat being so close and then my utter fuck up. What in the actual fuck was I thinking? I wasn't, that's the damn problem.

"I need to apologize. I feel awful." I groan as I drag my hands down my face.

Chapter Eight

Anya's perfect lips taste the same as they did the last time I kissed her all those years ago. Her soft moans send a surge of electricity through my veins, my core becomes molten as she takes me the way she knows I love. The moment her fingers wrap around my silky strands, memories of Clay doing something similar this morning slam into me and steal the air from my lungs.

Fuck. FUCK!

I abruptly pull away from her. Clay may have said he wouldn't care, but he's not here. I can't do this to him. He – I can't do this. "I – I can't do this." I repeat my thoughts aloud for Anya to hear. "This was a mistake. I shouldn't have come here. I can't do this to Clay." My movements are quick once I'm on my feet. Before she has a chance to respond, I rush to the door and slam it shut behind me harder than I mean to. My need to run outweighs the desire to be polite.

My fingers press against my lips as I walk to my car, tears continue to fall down my cheeks. Why does she still feel so good? My feelings for her shouldn't be as strong as they are. I love Clay. I am so in love with this man it's not even funny. How is it possible I'm having such desires for Anya of all people?

I drive home on autopilot with no memory of how I end up in the parking spot I'm sitting in. It takes a moment before I realize where I am, I find myself at the back entrance of Karma. The climb up the old rickety metal fire escape stairs that lead to Clay's apartment has me on edge. My heart beats erratically in my chest as I make my ascent to the door. Once I'm inside I collapse onto the soft cushions in the middle of the couch and curl up with a pillow wrapped tightly in my arms. I know in my heart I need to tell Clay, but I'm not quite ready to face him, especially not when he's got work for another few hours.

He may have said he was ok with her being involved, but he couldn't have been serious. There's no way, not with the history he knows we have. Damnit! Why did I go to her place today? I should have known better. The woman has only been my Roman fucking Empire for half a decade. When will I be able to move on from her?

I don't notice during my internal interrogation that the door from Clay's office entrance has opened. A throat clears which drags me out of my mental spiral, at least until I look up and see Anya standing before me. She's still wearing next to nothing with a crop top that barely covers her tits and those damn Anya bunny shorts from Buffy, that she knows used to drive me wild. My eyes go wide as I take her in.

"Kat," she says my name cautiously. Her anxiety at my potential reaction is clear. I swear to all things holy, I never used to be such a basket case. "Can we please talk?"

Anya slowly steps in my direction, putting one foot in front of the other as she closes the distance between us. Once she's on the couch next to me she begins speaking again.

"I didn't mean for that to happen. I'm so sorry. I know you're with Clay." Her voice cracks as she speaks, "I would never want to come in the middle of someone else's relationship."

My eyes find hers, the sincerity I find in them shocks me. She's serious, Anya is actually one hundred percent serious in this moment. The lack of control I have over myself right now should terrify me. Honestly, giving into what I've obviously wanted for so long makes me feel free, at least for a second. I throw the pillow on the floor and lunge for her. Once my lips find hers, my hands begin to tremble as they delve into her soft strands. I guide her face closer as I deepen the kiss. Our tongues battle for control and my hands slowly start to explore the contours of her luscious body.

I pull back just enough to nip Anya's swollen lower lip, sucking it into my mouth which elicits a loud, long, needy moan from this beautiful creature. My own whimper escapes when her hands find their way to my hair as she holds me in place, consuming me from below with a kiss that would make HawkHatesYou blush. I begin to grind against her thigh, my clit needing just a little friction and attention.

As soon as my fingers feel the soft exposed skin of her breast I jerk backward. A sudden realization hits me like an iceberg in the middle of the Atlantic and brings the pain I had run away from not more than an hour ago come rushing back. Fuck. "An, I can't do this with you. I'm with Clay. Oh my god." Tears prick at my eyes, but a sudden dark chuckle startles me. I glance over to where the noise came from to see Clay standing there with thick arms crossed over his chest.

"Kat, we had this conversation just this morning." His wicked smirk tells me he saw more than just me pulling away. Do I see desire in his eyes? No, that's not possible.

"Clay, I – I'm so sorry." I sob and scoot my ass as far from Anya as I can, like I'm a fucking teenager who just got caught making out with someone when we were supposed to be studying.

"Princess, I'm ok with you two being together." Clay's tone is so gentle and calm as he speaks, "As long as you're happy and you come home to me." His eyes find Anya's before he continues, his words are meant for me, but his gaze doesn't leave hers. He needs her to hear him as much as me. "And it's only with her, I'm not going to be upset about anything that you need to do for you. I'm not going anywhere baby. You're it for me."

Anya gasps when what he says sinks in. I glance in her direction to see the clear shock etched across her beautiful features. My emotions are all over the place. I can't keep my thoughts straight. A loud sob retches from my chest as I leap from the couch and rush past Clay running into our bedroom where I fall onto the bed, in the same damn position as last night.

Why is it that I can't deny her even after all this time? My heart lurches in my chest as so many thoughts rush through my mind. *He can't honestly mean he's ok with me being with someone else. That's how Hadley's relationship went up in flames. Though Andy was a dick. What if he changes his mind? What if... what if...what if....*

Can I really do this? Can we survive something like this if I do give into my own selfish desires?

Chapter Nine

Jesus fucking Christ. When I finally got a chance to get away from Tina after seeing Anya rush in here the way she did, I never expected to find the sight before me. The way Kat is writhing on top of Anya is hot as fuck. Is this how she is when she's with me? God damn, seeing Kat with her should infuriate me, but all I can see is just how much they care about each other. My Princess is just being stubborn as usual and refusing to hear me out. Whether it's because of me or because of Hadley's situation with Andy, I'm not one hundred percent sure.

"An, I can't do this with you. I'm with Clay. Oh my god." I can't help but chuckle when I hear Kat blame me for her reasoning for pushing Anya away. I can see the tears gleam in her eyes from here as she processes what she just did. Oh, my sweet Pickle.

"Kat, we had this conversation just this morning." My smirk must show my arousal because the expression on my girl's face is precious.

"Clay, I – I'm so sorry." She sobs and pushes herself to the edge of the couch putting as much distance as physically possible between her and Anya.

"Princess, I'm ok with you two being together." I try to keep my tone as gentle as I can, knowing she's punishing herself over this, "As long as you're happy and you come home to me." I train my gaze on Anya as I speak in hopes that she understands my next statement. "And it's only with her, I'm not going to be upset about anything that you need to do for you. I'm not going anywhere baby. You're it for me."

Anya's sharp inhale tells me she gets it, but the moment that Kat runs out, I breathe out a sigh of relief knowing I can have the conversation I want to before I take care of my girl. I move to the front of the couch and hover over Anya who is still seated on the couch. My eyes shoot daggers at the woman before me who has caused so much pain for the love of my life.

Never in my wildest dreams did I expect to have to share Kat when she finally agreed to be mine. But there isn't a damn thing I wouldn't do for her to keep her happy,even if it means welcoming in the cause of so much turmoil into our lives.

"Anya, I don't know exactly what caused you to leave her like you did, but I don't think you can comprehend what you left behind." I snarl at her, "what I had to help heal because you were too busy doing what?" My glare bores into her as I wait for a response.

As soon as she speaks, I feel like the biggest ass of all asses. Fuuuuc-cckkkk.

"It's no excuse. I should have been open with Kat before I just left like I did." She says tearfully after explaining her story. "Clay, I love her. I have been in love with her for the past seven years." She chokes out. "From the moment I walked into a class and saw her snacking from a lunch box filled with pickles in the middle of a fucking lecture hall."

I stare at her, unable to find words to speak.

"I don't want to come between you. I will stay away. I'm so sorry." She sniffs as she stands and tries to sneak past me.

"Anya, wait." I say before I turn toward her. "You're not coming between us if I'm not fighting this. As soon as I realized who you are, who you are to Pickle, a part of me knew that she would find her way to you. Just know, she and I, we're a package deal. So, you're going to need to keep that in mind before you make a decision."

"Clay, I – " she begins to speak but I cut her off.

"She'll come around; it's going to take time. You and I both know she's worth the wait if that's what you want." Frustrated with how this conversation has gone, I glare at her. "For now, just get out of here so I can talk to her. I'm sure you'll hear from one of us soon."

With a nod toward the door, she hurries out and disappears down the stairs. I let out an annoyed groan before I head toward our room with my sight set on the woman in my bed. As soon as I reach our room, I take in the vision before me. Kat is the most stunning woman I've ever seen. She may have tears streaking her cheeks at the moment matched with puffy red eyes from crying, but God damn. She's a goddess.

I step up to the bed and find myself in a similar position as last night, crouched beside the edge where she lay quietly sobbing.

"Kat, talk to me about what's going on in that beautiful brain of yours?" I ask gently. She shakes her head, unable to speak. My gaze rakes down her beautiful curves and back up to her face before I speak again. "Princess, I'm not going anywhere. I'm not mad. Talk to me." I urge her to get her concerns off her chest, so she doesn't implode.

"I'm so fucking scared, Clay. I love you more than anything, but my love for her hasn't gone anywhere either. I don't know what to do." She begins to sob even harder.

When I hear the anguish in her voice, I don't bother trying to stop myself. I climb into bed next to her and pull her into my arms. Once she's settled and tucked as tightly against me as she can possibly be, I break the silence.

"Babygirl, even if I have to share you, having only a part of your heart is better than having none of it. I love you, Kat. That's not going to change because you need to fulfill another part of your desires with someone that I don't want to compete with." I explain as delicately as I can. "As long as you want her, I will welcome her into our lives in whatever capacity the two of you choose."

There's nothing else to say. I know she's heard me when she buries her face in my neck. The only thing I can do now is help her realize she's not being selfish by wanting Anya too. Even if it's going to hurt me to see them together, at least for a while.

We lay in bed together for a long time, no words need to be said as we just lay here enjoying the closeness. Scenarios of what's to come flood my mind. I know Kat is going to give in, it's just a matter of time before she realizes it too. My arms wrap tightly around her as I pull her a little closer. *Princess, you are going to drive yourself crazy until you give into what you want.*

Chapter Ten

My phone dings from next to my spot on the bed causing my eyes to fly open. The coolness at my back tells me Clay is gone. I can't say I blame him. Hell, I can't believe what I did last night. He says he's ok with it, but how can he be? I'm feeling feisty already this morning with how frustrated I am with myself. Seeing the message from Ryan doesn't help since I know she was out with Jax last night.

Ryan

Mud House? Need Caffeine.

I snort to myself before I respond.

Kat

You gave him a mouth hug, didn't you?

Hadley

Oh. My. God! Say it's not true! Jax?! Of all peo-ple! This man has insisted on spending all of his money on strippers for years now!

Ryan

Don't worry, Moms. I didn't sleep with him. He dried me up before it could even get that far. He got to a solid second base before it ended.

My lips twist into a wicked grin as I type back my reply.

Kat

You poor thing. You need to get those cobwebs swept out from in there. Are you going to let me do it for you yet?

Hadley

Kat! LOL

Kat

What? I love Clay and all, but it's not like Ry and I haven't had sex before. I'd bang both of you if you'd let me. My girls are sexy!

Ryan

Obviously I was better than Clay if you're still bringing it up.

It's not that she was better than Clay. It's just that women are such a different experience altogether. A woman's body, her curves, her scent. God, there's nothing like it. While Clay can manhandle me and make me feel things I've never felt before, Anya is able to bring a sensuality to the table that I haven't had in so long.

Fuck. No, no no no. I didn't just think of her and Clay at the same time. Fuck me. What am I going to do? Crap!

Ryan

Can we please meet for coffee, you crazy bitch-es?

After I admonish myself for a few more minutes I throw the blanket off and sit up. Once I quickly stretch and wake up my limbs, I rush to the closet where I pull out my favorite sundress since It's supposed to be warm today. The light purple dress is so comfortable. Does it help that the neckline is plunging and gives me a confidence boost? Yes, absolutely. After the last forty-eight hours, I need all the help I can get so that I don't have to tell the girls everything that's happened. Ryan won't be able to keep this from Hadley and shit, Hadley just won't understand. Hell, I don't even understand what I want right now.

Hadley and I arrive at Mud House at the same time, her beautiful smile greets me as soon as she steps out of her car. The moment she closes the door she rushes to me and wraps her arms around me in an embrace that has me ready to spill everything.

"Hey babe! How are you?" She gushes while we walk toward the entrance.

"Hi, my love," I grin at her as warmly as I can. The affection I have for these two women is beyond anything I've ever felt for friends. Well, maybe not all friends. The thought of Clay brings a warmth to my heart. "I'm good. It's just been a long few days. I need some caffeine to get through whatever Ry is about to tell us."

Hadley giggles. "I can't believe you asked if she gave him a mouth hug!"

"Gave who a mouth hug?" Our friend Kayleigh asks as we approach the counter.

Hadley's face turns red, the embarrassment of being overheard talking about Kayleigh's husband's best friends. I can't help the chuckle that passes my lips as I wrap a loose arm around Had and turn back to our friend.

"Ryan and Jax hung out last night and –" Kay holds her hands up in front of her face, a sign for me to stop.

"Nope, that's enough. I don't need to know any of his extracurriculars with my friends. Thank you." She shivers dramatically like my admission has scarred her for life. "I'll have your coffees up in a minute as long as you never mention this to me again."

Hadley and I exchange an amused look before we burst into laughter. "Deal," I agree.

"Hey babes!" We hear Ryan call from behind us. I glance over my shoulder to see the knockout that is my former friend with benefits. Damn, she's gorgeous in her yoga pants and crop top. It's not until I see her boots that I groan out loud. Thankfully her brother Jack is here and calls her to him before she can see my apprehension.

"What's wrong?" Hadley asks me as we wait for our drinks.

"She's dressed to hike. I'm wearing a dress." I whine. Do I love to work out? Yes absolutely, I made it my profession after all. Do I love going where the bugs live? Not particularly.

"Holy fucking shit." Hadley whispers from next to me. Before I can respond she's rushing toward a large, tattooed man that I've never seen before. "GREYSON FREAKING MANCINI! When the hell did you get back into town?"

Oh shit, Ry.

My eyes land on her, the look of horror etched across her face nearly breaks me. She's told me about this guy. Her brother's best friend. She's had such a crush on him since she was in high school. Her face pales as she takes him in. It takes several minutes before she even speaks.

"Grey," his name is nearly inaudible.

I stand frozen as I take in the exchange. Once Ryan starts rambling, I make my way to where she stands with Greyson and wrap an arm around her waist. "Do I have to beg for an introduction, babygirl?" I toss my hair over my shoulder to show off my chest and bring his attention to me.

"Pickle, this is Grey." Ryan doesn't break contact with his face while she speaks, meanwhile I glare at the man. I know she's going to spiral. "Grey, Pickle. Well, Kat, but I call her Pickle because she hates it, and I think it's adorable. She made the mistake of telling me that was her nickname in college, and well, you know me. I always stick to a bit."

"Nice to meet you, Kat slash Pickle." Greyson smiles down at me and extends his hand for me to take. I nod without reciprocating the action.

"Uh-huh, well, we've got things to do." I gently pull Ryan along before I yell for Hadley to follow.

Ry starts spiraling the moment we get out to her jeep, just as I expected. She's ready to strangle Hadley, under the assumption that she knew Greyson was coming back. It's not until we finally arrive at the waterfall that she is obsessed with, that she finally relaxes. Ryan's tense stance eases as soon as she is testing her lens and lighting for this impromptu photoshoot. The moment I sense her stress dissipate I feel my own worries roar their ugly head.

My gaze is locked on the horizon as memories of the last two days unpack in my mind. I barely hear the click of the camera lens as I relive seeing Anya for the first time in half a decade all over again in my mind. She's as gorgeous as ever; her lips as sweet as honey and my god, her body has just gotten better with time.

When I agreed to go to her house, I never expected that kiss to happen. I just needed to hear her side of things. Maybe I was naive to think that nothing would happen when my feelings are obviously still so strong. I just never expected her to still feel the same.

"Pickle!" Ryan's voice cuts through the cacophony of noise in my head.

"Sorry, what's up?" I blink rapidly trying to expel the thoughts from my mind, at least for the moment.

"Are you ok? I've been calling your name for five minutes." Ryan's eyes are full of concern as she takes me in.

I wave her off and smile, "Maybe use my real name next time and not that damn nickname."

"Where's the fun in that?" She teases before she directs me to move in the position she's looking for.

The rest of the time we're together I allow myself to think of the what ifs. What if this makes everything go to shit for Clay and me?

What if Anya leaves again? What if – what if it works out and turns into something unexpectedly incredible?

As the afternoon sky begins to fade into evening we make our way back to Ryan's Jeep. I climb in the back seat and let Hadley sit up front. Before I can give myself any time to talk myself out of it, I grab my phone and tap out a quick text.

Kat:

> What is it that you want, An?

Unsurprisingly her response is almost instant.

Anya:

> You, Kat. From the moment I saw your picture on Clay's phone and realized I may see you again, I want you in any way you'll have me.

Kat:

> I won't give him up for you, Anya.

Anya:

> I'm not asking you too, Kat. I'd say I would be open to both of you but after yesterday, I'm pretty sure he wants my head on a spike.

> Kat, can I ask you – what is it that you want?

K at has been hiding behind her workouts and clients the past few days. I'm not sure what's happened between her and Anya since Anya was last here, but I know she needs to get out of her head. With the additional trainers on staff now, I was able to schedule us both off today. Once I pull out an appropriate outfit for Kat, I call for her to come into the bedroom. She walks in as I drag my sweatshirt over my head.

"What is it?" She asks as she leans cautiously against the door frame.

"Princess, get changed, we're going out." I gesture toward the clothes laying on the quilt.

"Why the hell would I wear that? It's hot out!" She whines in response.

"Just get changed, you'll see when we get there." I flash a smirk in her direction before slapping her ass as I leave the room. I chuckle under my breath when I hear her cursing my retreating form.

About forty minutes later we arrive at Xtreme sports, a complex that has a variety of extreme sports including what we're here for. I park my truck a few spots from the door before we both hop out. Kat rounds the front and arches a brow in my direction.

"You have been in your feelings since I walked in on the two of you. I know you've reached out to her." I admit part of my reason for bringing her here.

"So, you want to shoot me?" She asks, trying to hide her amusement.

"Yes, yes I do." I deadpan. "No, we're a team. But you still need to work out whatever is happening in that beautiful brain of yours. We figured this would be the best way for us to pull you out of it."

"We?" Kat's face screws up with confusion.

"Yes, we." A deep voice says from behind her. Kat spins quickly and squeals out in delight.

"Auggie! What are you doing here?"

"Hey, KitKat." He chuckles as he wraps her in a tight embrace. "This dumbass over here called when she came back. I knew violence would be the only way to get you out of your head."

His nefarious grin sends chills down my spine. Yeah, I'm going to need to get a straight answer out of her about what he does for a living.

"Let's go, kids." He smirks at me before he tucks Kat into his side and drags her along to the entrance.

We spend the next few hours playing paintball, game after game. The two of them take out our competition each time without batting an eye. In the end it's to the point that my presence is nearly irrelevant. Kat's face is brighter than it has been since Anya showed back up.

"So, KitKat. Are you going to fuck her or stick with this one?" Her brother asks nonchalantly.

"Bro, I'm right here." I groan while following the two of them back outside. AK throws his head back with an over-the-top laughter and flips me off as they continue putting distance between me and them.

I discreetly give them space. She needs perspective and he's probably the best one to give it to her given the circumstances. By the time they are saying goodbye, my body is feeling the beat down it's taken from the adrenaline of the games. AK waves as he gets on his motorcycle and tears off out of the parking lot.

Kat smiles up at me sweetly before pressing a soft kiss against my lips. "I love you, take me home and fuck me until I can't walk for a week."

My cock instantly swells in my pants, causing a pained groan to pass my lips, "Fuuuckk, Kat!"

I hear her giggle softly before she disappears into the truck. My eyes are locked on where she was just standing for a moment longer before I head to my side and hop in. The engine roars to life easily and we're off.

We've been on the road for only five minutes and I'm reciting the words from Eminem's 'Under the Influence.' When I get to that line – you know the one – Kat slides over and palms my stiff cock through my pants. I hiss out a breath and glance at her out of the corner of my eye. She's got a wicked grin dancing on her lips as she reaches over and frees my hard length.

"Princess, what are y –," she doesn't give me a chance to finish my question before she lowers herself and wraps her perfect pouty lips around my crown. "Fuck!"

I feel her smile just before she hollows her cheeks and sucks me in deeper. She lets out a soft moan around my dick, which feels so fucking good my hips involuntarily thrust up. Kat chokes around me, but doesn't let up. She continues to fuck me with her mouth as I drive home.

My hand wraps around her hair to keep it out of her face and keep a little control on her.

"God damn, Princess. You take me so fucking well." I moan before thrusting into her throat again. The sweet choking sound fills the cab of my truck again as tears begin to stream down her beautiful face. I barely get the truck into a parking spot and she releases me with an audible pop. "Kat! Fuck, I was so close baby." I complain.

"If I don't feel your cock inside my pussy right now, I'm going to scream. You and I both know you won't let me fuck you in the truck with a chance of someone seeing me." She winks before sliding out.

God damnit, why does she have to be right? I tuck myself back into my pants and exit the truck before I follow her up the back steps to the apartment. As soon as I'm inside she pushes me back against the wall. Kat's mouth crashes into mine, our lips fight for domination and control in the kiss. Her sweet soft tongue slides past when my lips part for a breath. I groan into her, my nails bite into her hips as I hold her close and grind against her belly. We're lost in a heated frenzy of lust. I don't realize she's dragged me to the couch until she shoves her hands against my chest forcing me back. I land on my ass; the soft cushions break my fall.

"What the hell has gotten into you?" I smirk up at her as she peels off her top. She wastes no time before she unclasps her bra and tosses it on the ground. Fuck, she's gorgeous, her tits are so full and perky. She's fucking perfect. My girl knows exactly how to get a rise out of me. When she knows I won't take my eyes off of her, she turns around and slowly drags her pants over her hips exposing the delicious peach of her ass. Kat kicks off her pants and turns back around. She kneels in front of me to help me remove my own bottoms.

The second they're gone, she's straddling my lap. Nothing between us but skin. Kat's slick cunt grinds against my hard length as she teases us both. I throw my head back against the back of the couch in frustration. I dig my fingers into her hips and attempt to guide her on but she refuses.

"Princess, my cock is throbbing. Please, take me. Use me however the fuck you want, but fucking fuck me." I beg. Yes, I am man enough to beg when she's tormenting me like this.

With a wild grin she hovers over me before lining myself with her entrance and quickly impales herself with my stiff cock. We both cry out in pleasure at the intense ecstasy. My hand finds her hair, I wrap it around my fist once, twice, before yanking just enough to get her attention.

"Fuck! Clay! Yes!" She sobs as she continues to use my dick for her own pleasure. I thrust up into her from below and her moans become louder. That's the moment she decides to play dirty. I feel her pussy constrict around my cock.

"Damn, Kat! You feel –" She does it again, I realize it's on purpose. Fuck. Me.

"I need to feel you claim this pussy, Baby." She whimpers as she clenches around me again while bouncing on my cock.

There's no way. Fuck. I groan and bring her lips to mine, sealing whatever the fuck this is with a kiss. Kat continues fucking me as tingles start at the base of my spine before exploding the next time she grips me.

This time I feel her convulsing around me which causes my cock to jerk inside her before filling her with my seed.

We're both panting by the time she finally releases me.

Her sweet face is right in front of me. I can see the concern in her eyes but before she can speak, I break the silence.

"So, you've decided you're going to give her a chance."

"How did you know?" She asks, thoroughly confused.

"Princess, you never take control and have me meeting god like you just did unless there is something you need to tell me that you don't think I'm going to like." I chuckle my way through the explanation.

"I'm so sorry." She responds quietly.

"Don't be. I know how much she means to you, but I'm not going anywhere. You're still mine." My lips meet hers in a soft chaste kiss.

"Always yours, Clay."

She presses her lips against mine again, this time the kiss is a little different, there's an urgency this time that wasn't there before. I pull away cautiously.

"What is it?" I ask.

"I know we've joked about having someone join us before, but what if..." she keeps her eyes on me as the words die on her lips.

"Kat, I don't trust her. The only reason I'm open to this is for you. Not for her." I snap.

"I know, and I appreciate that. But think about it..." Kat smirks at me with a knowing look before continuing. "Imagine if I were riding your cock like this..."

She pauses briefly before grinding down on me, my cock still half hard inside her. Fuccckkk.

"But we're on the bed and Anya is riding your face while she and I make out."

"God damnit, Kat," I groan as she begins to bounce on my cock once again.

"God damnit, Kat," I groan as she begins to bounce on my cock once again.

Chapter Twelve

Anya

Today has been chaotic as hell. Since the text from Kat came through, my mind has been a mess of every emotion there is. I haven't been able to settle on just one. She stopped responding to me when I asked what she wanted. Of course, I've been biting my nails since. I nearly fried a woman's hair after the exchange a few days ago.

"That's it, I'm tired of you looking like a wounded puppy. Lori, clear your schedule. We're taking our girl out." Axe announces from his station as he finishes sweeping up for the day. "Babe, go get changed and make yourself cute. There is that skimpy ass dress that we bought a few weeks ago. You're wearing that tonight, and all the men and women of Central Falls will be falling to their knees for a moment of your time."

"Yes! Let's get trashed and you can forget about your girl," Lori snorts.

Thirty minutes later, I admire just how good this dress looks on my tall muscular frame. A wrap style top barely covers my breasts and ties at my neck, the skirt part is cut short with a high slit that my hip bone sneaks out any time I take a step with my right foot. There's also sparkles, did I mention the sparkles?

My face is flawless, the full beat of makeup I applied has my confidence as high as Cheech and Chong. I smirk at my own reflection as the bedroom door slowly swings open. Axel pops his head in, and his jaw drops to the floor.

"God damn, woman!" My forever hype man. "You are going to have everyone eating out of the palm of your hands."

"I do look hot, don't I?"

"You're going to be all kinds of extra tonight now, aren't you?" Axe scoffs, the corner of his lips twitching as he tries to fight off his own amusement. "Let's get out of here, I told Lori we'd meet her in ten minutes."

"Why are we rushing? She's always late." I snort and grab my purse before following behind hm.

Sure enough we're at the bar for a good twenty minutes before Lori makes an appearance. Axel and I have already had one drink by the time she finds us. She's dressed in a sexy cropped tank that barely covers her breasts and a pair of leather pants.

"Well, god damn, woman." I shoot her a suggestive grin. "You look good enough to eat."

"Babe, we both know that you couldn't handle me." She teases and shoves my shoulder playfully.

Our evening is filled with drinks and dancing. I leave the two of them on the dance floor to make my way to the bar for another drink. My eyes lock with the bartender who nods in my direction to acknowledge my presence. I climb up on the stool in front of me as I wait for him to come back in my direction.

I feel a warm hard body graze my bare arm and sit next to me. I casually glance over and inwardly groan. He's cute, but he's going to make a pass at me and I don't want it. I may have come out looking like a whole ass meal, but damn. That was for me. I feel his eyes land on me a few times before I turn to face him and raise an eyebrow in question.

"I was just trying to buy a drink here, but you're very distracting." The handsome stranger winks at me.

"Does that really work for you?" I chuckle and wait for him to respond.

"I'm Greyson," his smile is warm and inviting as he holds out a hand and introduces himself.

I notice a man hovering at the back of the club in the shadows glaring at Greyson. Huh, it's not jealousy, it's rage. I wonder.

"Anya," I reply with a smirk. "And you're cute. But I asked you a question, does that line really work, Greyson?"

He leans in close and softly chuckles before replying. "You tell me?"

The closeness sends chills through my body, but not the kind I've felt with Kat.

"I think it could." I feel my cheeks flush as I reply and graze my nails down his chest to test my theory with the man that is still glaring at us and why Greyson approached me to begin with. "But, I'm," I pause as I search for the word, I don't want to lie. "Involved." That's not exactly lying is it?

"That's probably for the best. My best friend over there is already staring daggers into my head because his sister is in love with me and I'm over here with you." He smiles shyly like he's been caught.

Ahh this is all making sense now! I stare into his soul for a few moments before I reply softly so no one around us can hear. "Does he know that you're in love with her, too?"

"Shit, is it that obvious?" He asks as the color drains from his face.

"Babe, you flinched when I touched your chest like you only want one pair of hands on you." I wink at him.

He smiles sweetly, I can tell he's thinking of his girl.

"Fuck, I really want her, but he'll lose his mind. I've already lost enough people in my life. I don't want to lose my best friend too." He groans.

Oh, ok. I guess I'm involved in this conversation now.

"You could, I don't know. Tell him you have a thing for his sister and give him a heads up before you take that step with her. It's not always about the permission. It's about the acknowledgement."

"I guess I could do that. I don't even know if she wants to pursue anything with me." This guy is kind of adorable when he's questioning how to win his girl.

"Dude, go talk to your girl. Before you make any life altering decisions, tell her brother and then fuck her until she can't stand anymore." I groan with annoyance. He's adorable, but damn. I just told him what to do.

"Fuck it, alright. Hey. If you're down for some ink, I'll be at Alchemy Ink for a few weeks doing a guest spot if you want. My treat." His eyes are light with excitement.

"I have a girl for that, but thanks." I pat his shoulder before slipping off the chair and forgetting about the drink. "Have fun, Greyson. It was nice meeting you."

I sneak out of the club before anyone can stop me. This isn't my scene. I don't know what I was thinking.

My eyes flutter open way too early. I'm off today and it's time to make decisions in regard to what's going to happen here. I roll to my side and reach for my phone. It's only six in the morning, but knowing I'm not going back to sleep any time soon, I snatch the phone from the charger and tap my way around the screen and open my messages. I find Kat's contact and start typing up what I want to say.

Anya:

> Kat, I think we need to talk, in person. I will set up a plexiglass prison visiting room vibe if it makes you more comfortable.

> The more we ignore this, the harder it is going to be on everyone involved.

The exhaustion from last night still weighs heavily on my body and I collapse back down and cuddle into my blankets. A text bounces back a few minutes later.

I think I have an old rotary phone around here somewhere for my side of the glass so we can hear each other through the glass.

I snort at her response. Smartass.

I'll be there in an hour?

See you soon.

My heart constricts in my chest as I read the words again. She'll be here in an hour. Shit, I need to shower! I tear my covers off and rush into the bathroom. After I take the quickest shower ever – someone check the record books and call Guinness, I'm certain my name needs to be added. I rush back to my room and throw on a lounge set, it's pink and soft. Considering what happened the last time we were together, I don't want to push her. We need to actually talk.

As soon as I reach the bottom of the stairs there is a soft knock on the door. Unable to keep my cool, I rush over and open the door. Kat stands before me in a tiny tank top that her breasts are nearly popping out of and a pair of yoga pants that show every dip and curve of her muscular body.

Motherfucker, I'm screwed.

"Hey," Kat's smile is warm, as her eyes rake down my body I feel underdressed, even though I'm fully covered. "I brought coffee." She holds out a to-go cup from The Mud House.

"Thanks, you didn't have to..." I take a sip before I finish my sentence. "God, no I take it back, I need this every day." The flavor from the steaming liquid bursts on my tongue. Everything from the bean to what it's been roasted with is clear with every sip. "Damn, this is good coffee."

"I know, Kay is a master of her craft." She chuckles and lets herself in. "So, I couldn't find the rotary phone, is it ok if we just sit on the couch?"

After a long moment of silence, laughter erupts from my chest as soon as I realize what she is referring to.

"I guess that will have to do. I couldn't find plexiglass on such short notice anyways." I wink at her.

We both sit on the couch and nurse our drinks for a bit before either of us find the nerve to break the silence.

"Listen, Anya." Kat starts and I freeze. "I'm still hurt, I understand now why you left. Obviously, I'm not mad at why you left. We all write our own stories, and it wasn't the right time for you to add that plot twist for your parents."

Kat scoots forward and grasps my hand in hers. I gasp as my eyes lock on to hers, but I'm still unable to speak. So she continues.

"I'm glad that you made the choices you did. You still have your parents and I have Clay. The road to get to where we are now may have been bumpy, but look at what we both have now." She rushes on, "Even so, I've missed you every fucking day."

"I've missed you so much, Kat." I breathe out in a whisper.

"You asked me yesterday what I want." She smirks at me before she moves even closer and grips my chin before tilting my face so that my eyes meet hers. Our brilliant blue eyes fight for dominance once again. "I want both of you. I love him, but I've never stopped loving you too."

A single tear falls down my cheek.

She leans and presses her forehead against mine for less than a second when the front door crashes open, making us jump and sit up straight like we are a couple of kids getting caught on our parent's couch. Axel walks in and does a double take between the two of us and how close we are.

"God damn, Anya!" He smirks as he takes Kat in, "your description of your girl over the years did nothing to prepare me for the literal goddess before me."

Kat's cheeks flush bright red and she covers her eyes as she giggles. "Thanks, I think."

"Rick, behave." I roll my eyes. "Kat, this is Axel. Rick, Kat."

"I always behave, Louis." He winks at me. "It's nice to meet you, Kat. Also, sweetheart, I do vivids like no one can. You come see me when you need a touch up, don't trust your girl for that. She can't even do her own." Axel winks at her.

"Ewwww, David!" I do my best Alexis Rose impression before yelling, "Get out of here, ass!"

"OoO, is she loud?" He grins and waggles his brows at us.

"Oh my god!" Kat buries her face in her hands.

Axe's bellowing laughter is all we hear as he exits through the back door to get to the salon.

I drag her hands from her beautiful face and see the lingering embarrassment from his question. Without thinking, I gently grip her chin again and tilt her face to look at me. A soft smirk pulls at my lips when she finally looks at me.

Jesus, she's only gotten more beautiful over the years.

Almost like a switch has been flipped, this gorgeous creature is on top of me. She pushes me until my back is flush against the couch and straddles my thighs.

"Kat, we don't." I whisper, but just like when we were younger as soon as she sets her mind to something she doesn't let up. Her soft hands cup my cheeks as her lips find mine. I whimper into the kiss as soon as her tongue passes into my mouth. Fuck, I've missed this.

My arms instinctively wrap tight around her, her hips begin to grind against me, her pretty little pussy needing friction. She's just as turned on as I am. I nip at her swollen bottom lip and pull away from the kiss. The hunger in her eyes mirrors my own, my lips twitch into a knowing grin.

"Pick, if you don't get your ass in my room in the next five seconds, I will tear your clothes from your body and take you right here. I don't give a fuck if Axel comes back in here."

With an excited squeal she leaps off of my lap, I stand closely behind her. My fingers link with hers and I drag her to my room and quickly shut the door behind us.

Chapter Thirteen

My embarrassment faded in an instant when I saw the way Anya was looking at me. The way she used to devour me from across a room with just one glance. There's no way I could stop myself after seeing that look again after so long.

The bedroom door clicks behind me as I take in her room. Anya's style hasn't changed much, a bit more modern and mature, but she's still full of spunk. The black bedside tables are topped with fiery pink lamps with white shades. I chuckle softly, I guess her color palette has stayed the same.

Her strong arms wrap around my middle, and she presses her soft lips to my neck which sends chills through my body. Damn I've missed this, missed her. I lean my head back onto her shoulder to allow access. Anya nips at my sensitive skin which has me crying out with pleasure. I spin to face her and push her back until her legs are against the foot of the bed. My lips find the little bit of skin popping out from under that oversized shirt. Anya's body quivers at the intimate familiarity.

With a wicked grin, I back away just enough to drag the shirt over her head. Her breasts are being restrained by a black lace bra. I begin to salivate at the sight before me.

"An," I whisper. "How have you become even more beautiful?"

My hands press firmly against her shoulders, guiding her back into the mattress, right where I want her. I straddle her hips, letting her know exactly who's in charge. Holding her wrists in one hand, I use the other to cup her face, pressing my mouth against her perfectly pouty lips once again. Within seconds we're both lost in the kiss, lust and desire thick in the air around us. The moment her tongue parts my lips, I suck gently, making her release a moan from deep in her chest.

Chills wrack my body with each little noise that escapes her. My left hand caresses her back as I make my way to her neck. Once I have her hair wrapped around my fist, I tug so that her neck is fully exposed. My mouth latches on as I explore the space that used to drive her out of her mind. Meanwhile, my right hand gingerly unclasps the black lace barrier. Anya's gasp at the sudden release pulls a dark chuckle from deep inside me.

"Pick, please," she whimpers.

Instead of using my words, I use my body to respond. Once her bra is no longer in the way I grip her neck, pressing firmly against the pulse points. She cries out with need; Anya has always enjoyed a little forcefulness in the bedroom. My lips twitch up into a grin as I guide her onto her back, my face lowering to her breasts. Fuck her tits are perfect, my lips part and I swipe my tongue against the pebbled peak. She hisses at the sudden contact. I smirk at her response and gently nip on the sensitive bud.

"Kat," she whines.

"Shh, Bunny," I reply.

This time when I part my lips I latch on, sucking her nipple into my mouth so hard she screams at the intensity.

"Fuck me, yes!" Anya's reaction to my mouth on her tit has my pussy pulsing with its own need. God damnit, I need to taste her.

With an audible pop, I release her. I leave her quivering on the mattress as I shimmy down her body to get to her sweatpants. I hook my fingers under the waistband and slide them down her legs. She's completely bare, her arousal glistening along her folds the moment she's exposed.

Somehow, I keep myself from just diving in for a taste. Anya's eyes are dark with lust and desire. The moment I see her chew on her bottom lip, I nearly combust. Jesus, why is that so sexy? I press my lips against the inside of her thigh and she gasps. Slowly, cautiously I continue trailing kisses along her creamy skin until my mouth has found its way home.

My tongue darts out and swipes her length, swirling quickly around her clit. Her tangy sweetness explodes across my tastebuds. We both moan in unison. She tastes even better than I remember. *Clay won't want to come up for air if he gets a taste.* My eyes lock on her face as I repeat the motion. Anya, obviously unamused by my teasing, tangles her fingers in my long locks and glares down at me between her legs.

"If you don't stop fucking around..." Anya begins to threaten me, and I cock a brow at her. My lips turn up in a vicious grin. She knows I will make her wait for it if she tries to tell me what to do. When she realizes what I'm thinking, she changes tactics and begins to beg. "My body is on fire, I need you. Please!"

Well, since you asked so nicely.

I slide a finger inside her tight cunt. Anya's hips buck and slam her pussy into my face. I chuckle and continue my torturous assault on her clit. I slide a second finger in, stretching her entrance just a little. She's so fucking tight. My fingers find that sweet spot inside and I begin to make the come-hither motion against her g-spot.

"Oh fuck! Kat!" She cries out as her body begins to convulse. I latch on to her clit, sucking the sensitive bundle of nerves hard between my lips as soon as her pussy begins to pulse around my fingers. "Fuck!!!" She screams as a gush of wet heat streams down my wrist. I slowly release her clit and press a soft kiss against her sensitive mound. A proud grin spreads across my face.

Clay would have so much fun with her.

"There is some supernatural power in that pussy because this is not why I came over here." I tease her as I lick my lips and climb back up the bed until I lay next to her.

"Mist-i-ca squir-ti-ca" She chants as she waggles her eyebrows at me.

We both burst into a fit of laughter as we lay in each other's arms.

My hair is still damp from the shower at Anya's as I walk into Clay's office. He's sitting in front of the computer with a frustrated expression on his face. Shit. Fuck. It's not that I feel guilty about what I did. I wish he was there, but I also don't want to drown him in my good time if he's in a mood.

"Princess," he says before I even fully step inside.

"Hey," I smile at him as I close the door softly. The moment he looks up at me, his eyes become heated. "What's going on?"

He's on his feet in a second and pins me against the door. He breathes me in and smirks.

"That can wait, you smell like her," a wicked smile plays on his lips as he darts his tongue out and licks my lips. My eyes go wide and I whimper. Shit, he said he was ok with this. "Fuck, I can taste her on you."

"I – I thought – I thought you…" I stammer.

"She tastes good." He winks at me before his lips crash against mine in a heated kiss that can only be described as him claiming me as his again. My knees tremble at the passion unleashed between us. By the time he pulls away, his arms have snaked around my waist and he holds me upright.

"Jesus, Mary, Joseph and the camel. That was…" the words die on my tongue as I keep my eyes on him.

"That was me telling you we're ok." He winks at me. "I love you, Princess."

I smile lovingly up into his beautiful golden eyes. How in the hell did I get so lucky? Clay holds me against his steady frame until I find my footing again. Once I'm able to stand up, he keeps his gaze trained on mine.

"What?" I ask.

"You look like you want to say something. I don't need details. As long as you're happy, I'm happy." He smiles warmly at me.

"Oh, I mean I am. It was…" I stop myself. I don't know how she'd feel about me sharing those details with him. "…It's just that I wish –" I cut myself off. Am I asking too much?

"You wish what?" Clays calming voice breaks through my thoughts.

"That you were there." I admit quietly, "Don't get me wrong, it was incredible. It seems my body craves both of you. And the idea of you tasting her with me had my pussy spasming while I…well."

Clay's shoulders lift and drop dramatically as he lets out a heavy sigh. Oh god, here it comes, he's going to leave me.

"Princess. Do I think it's hot as hell the thought of sharing you with a woman? Yes, of course I do. But remember, I was there when she broke you. Just because I'm ok with you being with her, doesn't mean I want her. I can still see you the morning you woke up on the bathroom floor." He shares his perspective, and it breaks me a little inside. "It's going to take a while for me to be able to trust her not to hurt you."

"I love you. I'm sorry, this is hurting you." Tears begin to fill my eyes.

"Don't you dare, Princess." Clay scolds, his fingers firmly grip my chin as he brings my gaze to meet his. There is a fire in his eyes as he speaks, "I told you to do this. I want this for you because I know as much as you love me, you've never stopped loving her."

Chapter Fourteen

Beads of sweat trickle down my chest and back with every move I make. The past thirty minutes I've been kicking the shit out of this punching bag. My hands are going to be sore as hell tomorrow with just how hard I've been going. My heart hurt when I saw the sadness in her eyes when she thought I was mad at her for doing what I told her to. She's still so broken over this bitch no matter what I do to help her.

With one final fist landing hard on the bag, I tear my gloves off and toss them to the ground. Kat being in a class right now is the only way

I'm going to get out of here without her noticing how worked up I am. My feet move fast and hard against the sidewalk as I weave in and out of pedestrian traffic, each step takes me closer to putting an end to her pain.

The run to Capelli Studio takes less than ten minutes. As soon as I rush into the front door of the salon, I spot Anya. She's standing behind her chair as she sweeps up the clippings from her last client. A man from the station next to her speaks, which drags my attention from her.

"Hello, Sir. Welcome to Capelli Studio, do you have an appointment?" His voice is very pleasant even though his gaze is questioning. Shit, I don't have a shirt on.

"Anya, may I please speak with you?" I direct my response to her as I stuff my hands in my short pockets. Her head whips up as she stares in my direction. Her eyes go wide when she realizes it's me.

"Clay, I – um. Sure." She leans the broom next to her station top and walks toward me. "Let's go back to my place so we can have some privacy."

"Louis," the man who greeted me calls the name out, his voice full of worry. Anya stops and turns back to him.

"It's fine, Rick." She responds – wait. Louis? What? Anya waves the man off and continues to lead me out the back of the building.

As soon as we enter her house and she closes the door behind us, I turn to face her. I take a breath to gather my thoughts before diving into what I need to say to the woman in front of me.

"The day I met her, she was broken and so wasted she couldn't stand." I begin.

"Clay, I don't," she starts, but I hold a hand up in warning.

"You're going to listen to what I have to say, Anya." I growl. "She had finished a bottle of Jameson and Becca was so concerned about how much she drank she was terrified to leave her alone."

I keep my eyes trained on her as I allow my words to marinade for several seconds before I continue.

"Becca couldn't stand straight, let alone watch over her. So, I stayed up the entire night watching Kat sleep on a bathroom floor because after she vomited the first time, she refused to allow me to help her to her room." I see the tears forming in Anya's eyes as I speak. Good, she needs to understand what her actions caused. No matter why she did what she did when she left. The only way I know she won't hurt her again is if she knows just how badly her vanishing act affected Kat the first time around. "I sat with my back against the tub all night to make sure she was ok. It took Kat months. MONTHS!" I shout the word when I repeat it.

"Clay. I swear to you –" she starts but I continue speaking over her.

"She wouldn't talk to anyone but me for months and even then, it was just because I wouldn't leave her alone. Anya, she never once uttered your name until she saw you again." I let out a heavy sigh. "I don't need you to apologize to me. That's not what I came here for. She wants both of us and I won't be the one to deny her that."

A tear falls down Anya's cheek. I step forward and wipe it away with my thumb.

"Clay, I love her. I never meant for any of this to happen." She whispers. "My reasons were valid at the time. But if I knew how bad of a time she was having, I would have come back. I will never forgive myself for the pain I have caused her."

"I want to believe that, but Anya." I sigh and walk through the kitchen into the living room. I make myself at home and sit on her couch. I bury my face in my hands for a moment before I glance up at her. "She hasn't had a serious relationship since you, until me, and that was after six years of me waiting to make a move."

"Well, at least I know you have stamina." She snorts and then covers her mouth shaking her head in embarrassment.

I can't help but chuckle. "I can see why she likes you." I roll my eyes.

"Seriously, Clay." Anya sits on the couch next to me, "I'm not leaving. Never again."

"Alright. Fine." I focus on her face, watching for any sign of hesitation or that she's going to run. "I told you; I'm not going to be the one to deny her what she wants. But what she wants is us, so..."

"So, what? She has us both." Anya's brow furrows with confusion. *She's fucking adorable.*

"Really?" I cock a brow at her and wait for it to click.

"Oh!" She gasps and I see the light bulb go off as soon as it registers. "You mean together."

We sit in silence as she takes me in. I feel exposed, granted I am shirtless but still. By the time she responds I need to head back to Karma to close up. I realize I left my phone back at the gym, Kat is going to be frantic. Fuck. I take Anya's hand and squeeze, she cocks a brow at me as I stand.

"I'll see you soon." My lips twitch as I fight a grin as I head out her front door.

Chapter Fifteen

Clouds of steam billow above my head as I stand under the scorching flow of water. The heat works out the soreness in my muscles. The stress of the past few days and making my decision to take things to the next level with Anya has taken its toll on my body. Don't get me wrong, I wouldn't change a damn thing because being with her was everything and more than it was back when we tried it before. I just, I don't know. Clay has seemed off since I mentioned I wish he were there experiencing it with me.

With a frustrated groan, I finish washing the day of sweat off my skin and shut the water off. I step out and wrap a towel around my naked body, the warm air surrounding me is cold compared to the heat of my shower. I let out a deep sigh and walk into the hall before I turn toward the bedroom. I notice a figure in the living room. I shriek in surprise, realizing only a moment later that it's Clay lounging on the couch, freshly showered as well.

"Hey, where were you?" I ask as I saunter over to him with a little extra bounce in my step.

"I had to run out for a bit, but I showered downstairs when I realized you were having a meeting with Lucifer." He smirks as soon as I start walking toward him.

"I feel attacked, but I've also seen that show and baby, I love you, – but smash!" I giggle.

His eyes darken as his gaze rakes up and down the length of my body. I feel the heat rush to my core. Jesus, this man does things to me. Feeling brazen, I drop to my knees before him. With my hands placed firmly on his thighs I push them apart to allow myself access. As soon as he allows me between his legs, I slip my fingers under the waistband of his shorts. My brow raised in a silent question. His lips twitch into a lopsided grin and he lifts his hips allowing me to tug the shorts off. The moment his cock springs free, my mouth waters with anticipation. The towel loosens around my chest and falls to the floor, forgotten in the moment.

My tongue darts out as I bow my head and lap up the precum glistening at his tip. He groans as his head falls back onto the couch. My lips part as I take his crown in, sucking gently. My cheeks hollow as I take him further into my mouth until I feel him at the back of my throat. My tongue curves around his shaft as I start to bob.

A soft gasp pulls my attention and I sit up, releasing Clay's cock with an audible pop. He groans, a mixture of frustration and anticipation appear on his face before he masks his emotions. His hand caresses my cheek as we both look in the direction of the noise. Anya is standing at the door with an unsure expression on her face. I smirk at her and arch a brow in invitation before I turn back to continue pleasing my man.

Clay's guttural moan as I take him into my throat again has my pussy dripping. I hope Anya hasn't left because the thought of her being here for this is making it even hotter. Clay's hands cup the back of my head as he thrusts into my throat again, which makes me choke around his cock. My gagging noises fill the room. Fuck, that's hot. A moment later I feel soft, delicate fingers caressing my bare ass. I moan loudly at the unexpected touch which only makes Clay thrust into my throat again.

Anya's hands are cupping my ass, massaging firm circles on each side before she changes her position. She spreads my legs and pulls my ass up into the air. Before I have a moment to comprehend what's happening, I feel her tongue flick against the tight ring of muscle. I cry out around Clay's cock which just makes him respond even louder. Anya chuckles against my skin as she swipes her tongue against my tight hole. She's never done this to me, my brain is a mix of uncertainty while my pussy is dripping even more as she continues the delicious assault. Suddenly a finger enters my pussy, pumping at an infuriatingly slow pace, her tongue matches the rhythm as she prods the sensitive hole. My nails dig into Clay's thighs, every nerve ending on full alert. I cry out when she finds my G-spot as she's tonguing my ass. I find myself on the brink of my climax when Clay's hands hold my head as he thrusts into me one more time, his cock swells as he finds his release. The moment he calls out my name as ropes of cum fill my throat sends me over the edge. Anya doesn't stop until she feels me come down from my own high, which only extends my release.

I release Clay from my mouth, Anya's fingers disappear from my pussy. I sit up and turn to face her, my lips find hers in an instant. My hands cup her neck as I deepen the kiss. She moans softly into me. We separate after a moment, and I turn to Clay who has an amused smirk on his face. I raise myself to wrap my arms around his neck and pull him to meet me, our lips lock and our tongues tangle in a dizzying exchange.

Anya's hands glide softly up my sides, pulling my attention back to her. I end the kiss and look between the two of them.

"What is it, Princess?" Clay asks, his voice low.

I shake my head, unable to say the words.

"Pickle, say what you want." Anya scolds as she tweaks my nipple which makes me whimper.

"I want you both. I want you to fuck me," I look at Clay briefly before turning back to Anya. "While I eat your pussy until you can't see straight."

Anya's eyes widen and I feel Clay stiffen next to me.

"If I knew having her here would bring out that kind of language, I would have insisted she stay the first night." His husky voice sends shivers through my body. "What do you say, Anya?"

"I say, where the fuck is the bedroom?" Anya stands and helps me to my feet. Clay isn't far behind in standing before he steps around us to lead the way to our bedroom.

Their enthusiasm makes me laugh.

Chapter Sixteen

Anya

My body is still as stone as I sit on the couch turning the key over in my hand. Clay gave me a key to his apartment with Kat. I've not moved since he left twenty minutes ago, the back door swings open smashing against the wall. I see Axe rush toward me out of my peripheral which drags me from my thoughts.

"What the hell, Rick!" I shout at him.

"Don't you what the hell me, are you ok? You never came back, and you haven't been answering your phone!" He yells back at me.

I pull my phone out of my pocket and see five missed calls. Oops, I turn toward him and hold my hand out palm up to show him the key.

"You're moving out?" He gasps and clutches his chest.

"No, you idiot! Clay gave me a key to their place." I spout back as I stand and begin to pace back and forth until there is an indent in the floor.

"So, he's giving you a green light to come over any time and you're still here?" Axel's question is laced with amusement.

I glare at him and drag my hands through my hair. What the hell am I supposed to do with this? The man obviously doesn't like me. I may understand why; had I known the pain I caused her, I would have come back sooner to make it right. But do I really want to put myself in this position without talking to Kat about it? My eyes fly to Axe, his Cheshire grin has my stomach twisting.

"He made it clear that he hates me for hurting her," I whine.

"An, it seems like this may be his way of giving you an in. I wasn't here for the conversation, but if this is what Kat wants, this may be his way of giving her and you that chance to rekindle things while the two of them are together." Axel stands next to me and wraps me in a quick hug. "Not everything is black and white. You can date her while she dates him. Who the hell knows what may happen long term between the three of you."

"I hate when you're right," I groan into his chest.

"Which explains why you're still here all these years later." He winks as he releases me, "Now get the hell out of here and go have some fun."

I can't believe that just happened. Kat's fingers are tangled around mine as she and Clay lead me down a hallway until we enter a bedroom. It's a large bed. It could easily fit four people. Clay steps aside and drags his shirt off to expose an insanely muscular chest. Holy shit, this is actually happening. Jesus, I could tell he was muscular, but God damn his body is beautiful. My jaw hits the floor as I take in the Adonis before me. Channing Tatum circa Magic Mike One, has nothing on this man.

"Ok, I get it." I say to no one in particular.

Kat starts giggling as she spins me to face her. Our mouths collide and tongues tangle in a kiss that has my knees buckling. Kat holds me tight against her to keep me on my feet. Our mouths still fused together, she hooks her fingers under my top and pulls it over my head. Her nimble fingers have my pants around my ankles in seconds. When she releases me, I hear a sharp intake of breath from beside us.

"Fuck, yea...I get it too." Clay chuckles darkly as he grips his cock.

I turn to him with a smirk tugging at my lips and wink at him. Maybe this was a good idea. Kat's hand grips my hip as she presses a soft kiss against my collarbone. I whimper at the sensation her lips cause any time they are on me. She pulls me against her as her other hand softly travels down my side, around my stomach and eventually she finds her way to the apex of my thighs. Kat's fingers expertly dip between my folds to find just how wet I am. Her shoulders shake with dark amusement before she speaks.

"Lay down and spread your legs. I want him to see how you glisten for me." This dominant side of her is more than what it was before. She's come into her own even more in the years we've been apart.

I step around her as Clay closes the distance between them and wraps himself around her. Seeing them kiss should make me uncomfortable, shouldn't it? Why does it make me want them both right now? Fuck, what is happening? I do as she asks and spread myself before the two of them. Clay's hand is still fisting his cock as they part and take me in. A hunger in both of their eyes has my pulse humming.

"Jesus Christ, I thought the way you drench the sheets was wild, Princess." Clay's whiskey smooth voice makes me squirm, "You're going to drown."

"What a way to go though." Kat giggles as she climbs on top of me.

Her lips find mine again, the kiss is full of heat and lust. A passion we've shared for so long ignites any time we're near even though we've only found each other again recently. She slowly trails hot wet kisses down my body until she is between my thighs.

"An," she whispers as she blows a hot breath against my clit, making my skin erupt with goosebumps. All I can do is whimper in response to the anticipation. "I want you to keep your eyes on him when you come. Can you do that for me, Bunny? Can you let him see how beautiful you are when you come on my face?"

There's no point in fighting it, she knows she has every bit of control over me in the bedroom. I nod my head in agreement. I'll do whatever the fuck she wants if it means she's mine. Ours. I glance up at Clay who is hovering behind Kat. His hands are caressing her ass cheeks as she swipes her tongue through my folds, up my length until she's swirling around my clit.

Oh, fuck.

"Kat!" I sob, my hands fist the sheets below me as she holds my thighs wide. I throw my head back against the mattress and squeeze my eyes closed as she has me climbing high. Suddenly, she stops and my eyes fly open, I glance down at her. A wicked smile on her face,

"Eyes on Clay, Bunny." She gently nips my clit before diving back in. It takes all of my energy and effort to keep my eyes open.

The moment Clay enters Kat, she moans against my cunt which makes my pussy spasm. I cry out and thrust my hips forward, grinding my mound against her tongue. She grips my thighs harder to keep me in place. Once she feels I'm under her control, she releases one thigh to slide two of her delicate fingers inside me. I whimper at the intrusion; she feels so good inside my pussy. I never want this feeling to end.

As soon as Clay finds a rhythm Kat likes, she begins to work me even harder. I sob with my eyes locked on his, Kat sucks my clit between her lips hard and I see stars. My pussy convulses around her fingers, but she doesn't let up as I reach the crescendo of my pleasure.

Chapter Seventeen

Clay's finger presses against the tight ring of muscle as he pounds his cock into my pussy. Evidence of my arousal drips down my thighs. His balls slap against my clit as he fucks me, edging me closer to another release. I grin against Anya's cunt as she comes down from her first orgasm, allowing just a moment to breathe before I shove my tongue as deep into her pussy as I can. She cries out at the unexpected penetration. I swirl it in circles while inside her, tasting the sweetness left from her climax. Anya squirms under me, I wrap my arms tight around her thighs again to keep her still before I glance up and lock onto her gaze.

"You can give me another one, Babygirl." I say once her eyes meet mine.

She whimpers as I bury my face between her legs, my tongue stroking her sensitive bundle of nerves with practiced flicks. Just the right amount of pressure to drive her wild. I can tell the moment Clay sees her body tense as another orgasm begins to take hold. I slide my fingers inside her as my tongue continues its perfect rhythm of flicks and swirls against her clit. Her hips buck as she feels the intrusion. Anya's hands dig into my scalp as she holds me in the position she wants, I flatten my tongue for her to use as she grinds her pussy against me chasing her release.

"Jesus, Kat! I'm coming!" She sobs, her fingers seek purchase as she tangles my hair in her hands.

Her reaction to the second orgasm makes my pussy convulse, squeezing Clay's cock which elicits a loud groan from my man.

"God damnit, Princess!" Clays fingers dig into my hips so deliciously hard I know I'm going to have bruises. His thrusts become erratic as his cock swells inside me. Knowing that little move sends him over the edge has my clit throbbing. His arm wraps around me and he pinches my clit between his fingers as he empties himself inside me. My orgasm is explosive as my cunt pulses around him until we're both sated.

I flinch as Clay pulls out; my pussy tender and sore from the pounding, but deliciously so. Before I can stand on unsteady legs, Clay lifts me into his arms and places me on the bed next to Anya. I grin at her, a mischievous look in her gaze.

"What's happening in that head of yours?" I ask.

She doesn't speak with words; Anya shimmies down the bed and forcefully parts my legs. A loud moan escapes when I feel her tongue lapping up the mixture of my and Clay's releases. I hear a low husky groan from where Clay lays next to me as Anya latches onto my clit. A mixture of sucks, nips and swirls send me over the edge so quickly I see stars.

I can smell the pizza before Clay returns to the room. Fuck, I'm hungry. I'm not sure which is a more welcome sight, Clay baring food after a sex marathon or the fact that he's only wearing a pair of shorts. Anya and I are cuddling as we lean against the headboard. He carefully places the box on the quilt as he hands us each a paper plate.

"I will spank both of you if you get any grease on these sheets." He mumbles under his breath.

"What was that, Magic Mike? I couldn't hear you over your shirtless abs." Anya teases him and playfully sticks her tongue out at him.

Clay rolls his eyes before he sits on the other side of me. I drape my leg over his and enjoy the silence as we all enjoy a slice of pizza.

"So, is this really going to be a thing? We can keep doing this?" I ask, unable to hide the hopefulness in my voice. I glance between the two of them as I wait for a response.

"Princess, I'm down for anything you want. Especially if you're going to become bossy like that." Clay's voice is soft yet filled with lust as he responds.

"Anything that means I get a small piece of you." Anya whispers against my temple before pressing a soft kiss into my hair.

I grin wickedly. "What about..."

"We're not there yet, Princess." Clay interrupts me before I can finish my thought.

How rude! I internally whine, though I know he's right. There's a good chance they'll never be ready for more than what just happened. I will have to be ok with that. Yet, the idea of seeing the two of them getting lost in one another has my pussy dripping all over again.

Chapter Eighteen

T wo weeks later

Knowing what I was going to come home to this evening made my day drag. Everyone that came into Karma today had questions. Even clients who are there daily decided today was the day that they needed to talk to me about how they can improve. I know I sound like an ungrateful ass right now.

This is the first time that Kat and I have been alone without Anya. Don't get me wrong, Kat has always been a firecracker in bed, but Jesus Christ, this woman turns into a porn star when the three of us are together. She's so dominant with Anya, it's hot as fuck to see. But I do miss the time alone with her.

"Princess," I call for Kat who is in the bedroom getting changed after a shower.

"Yea?" She pokes her head out to respond.

"Quesadillas for dinner?"

"Yes! Extra veggies please!" She exclaims as she returns to view with just the T-shirt on.

My eyes rake up and down her gorgeous body, she smirks as I take her in. The fact that she can act innocent when she knows damn well what she's doing to me shouldn't be such a turn on, but of course everything she does is a fucking turn on. I groan and turn back to the stove determined not to start another fire.

Kat sits on the counter watching as I cook just like she did that first time we messed around. It's hard to believe it's been over a year. She's got her gaze locked on me when I turn around to plate our dinner.

"What?" I ask while carefully placing our quesadillas on the plates I set on the counter before I started cooking. My eyes are trained on her while I cautiously move around where she's seated on the counter to grab sour cream and guacamole from the fridge.

"I love you, that's all." She smiles brightly at me.

"I love you too, Princess." I reply with a furrow to my brow. My ability to sense something more when it comes to her hiding things has become more potent since we began dating. "But..." I pry.

"I was just thinking about revisiting something." Her smile becomes wicked.

Oh hell. The experience with the two of them has been unbelievable in the best way but, am I ready for more? Is Anya ready for more? Fuck. She's funny as hell and just as sexy. Is that enough after just how much anger I had and probably still have for her? Though, a good hate fuck could be fun.

"Kat." I scold, my attempt to keep her from going where she's trying to go is an epic failure yet again.

"Baby! I know you like when you see her come because you grip my hips so hard, I have bruises. Not no mention the way that you fuck me even harder to the point I see stars even more than before she joined us." She argues her point.

I make myself busy and carry the plates to the living room where we have an episode of The Big Bang Theory ready to play. Dinner, just the two of us while we cuddle on the couch, nothing could be better than that. Ok well, something could be a little better.

"Princess, you don't even know if she can tolerate being around me without you." I reply dryly.

She rushes over to where I stand and pulls me down to sit with her. With a mischievous smile on her face, she asks.

"If she agreed to have a night just the two of you without me, would you try?" She asks as she taps away on her phone screen, I didn't even realize she had it in her hand.

"Sure, if she wants to spend some one-on-one time with me, I'm down. But don't push her."

She grins as she shows me her phone.

"I didn't need to."

Kat:

Hey, Bunny. I have a question for you.

Anya:

> Should I be concerned?

I glare at Kat which just makes her giggle before I continue reading the exchange.

Kat:

> What do you think about you and Clay having a date?

Anya:

> What do you mean?

Kat:

> Just the two of you. I'll catch up with Ryan and Hadley. You two can do something together, just the two of you and see what happens.

Anya:

> Is this his idea or yours?

Kat:

> Yes

Anya:

> You're a pain in the ass, Pickle. Yes, I'm in.

Fuck.

I shake my head and look at Kat. She's so proud of herself and I'm worried that Anya is only doing this to appease her.

"Sit, eat. Our food is getting cold." I say as I take a bite of my own meal.

We've been watching the show for a little over an hour. Kat's asleep on my lap, unease over this entire thing with Anya has my stomach in knots. Would I be into the three of us being a thing, sure. But I laid into

Anya hard about how she treated Kat when they split up. Will she be able to move past that? I pull my own phone from my pocket and start a new message. I've had her number since the morning after our first night together as the three of us. But I've never used it, until now.

Clay:

> Hey

Anya:

> Hi, Magic Mike.

I chuckle softly at her nickname for me.

Clay:

> Listen, we don't have to do this if you're not comfortable. I know she's being a bit pushy. It's fine how it is if that's what you want.

This response doesn't come as quickly. I sit tapping my fingers against my thigh while Sheldon is going off about his spot on the television screen when her reply comes through.

Anya:

> Yea, she is being pushy, but I wouldn't say yes if I really didn't want to.

Clay:

> Yea? Ok. I'll talk to you soon then.

Chapter Nineteen

G iven none of us know what to expect tomorrow, seeing as it's all of our first tattoo's; the girls and I decided to have a night in with snacks, wine, and rom-coms circa 1980's through the 90's. Don't judge us, ok. There is just something about watching *Pretty Woman* and then *10 Things I Hate About You* that is refreshing to the soul.

Hadley and Ryan are on their second shared bottle of wine, meanwhile I'm still nursing my first glass. Truthfully, I'm afraid to drink and let down my guard enough to tell them what's going on with Anya. I haven't figured out how to tell Hadley and until I know if this is going to be more than just sex, what's the point?

"Howya, ladies." Connor calls from the front door. A quiet shuffle sounds before he appears with his shoes in his hand and black suit jacket over his arm.

"Hey Con!" Ryan and I say simultaneously.

"Mo ghrá," Connor murmurs as he takes Hadley in like she hung the sun, moon, and stars. It's sickeningly sweet.

Though, Clay looks at me that way too. I just hope maybe one day he will look at Anya the same. Connor and Hadley get swept up in each other for a while. Feeling left out, I tug Ryan into my side to cuddle while we watch whatever is on the screen. By the time they come up for air, the movie is over and Ry and I are debating over the next one.

"Why not *St. Elmo's Fire*? We all love young Rob Lowe, right?" I offer as my suggestion.

"Yes, which is why we should watch *About Last Night*." She sasses me back.

We're glaring at each other when Hadley clears her throat, interrupting us with her solution. "You're both staying here so we can watch both. Now, quit acting like an old married couple."

"Babe, we would kill each other, besides she's getting dicked down so good she doesn't need it." Ryan waggles her brows at me as she responds to Hadley. "Did you see how she hobbled in here? She's walking as if she's been jackhammered all night."

"Oh my god, you did not!" Hadley snorts.

I bring my hands up to cover my face and shake my head. My skin heats with embarrassment. I mean she's not wrong, but damn, is it that obvious?

"Why are we friends?" I glare at Ryan again.

"Because you love me, even when we bicker." She presses a soft kiss against my lips like she always has when we are close like this. My body goes rigid; Ry cocks a brow with a silent question. I subtly shake my head telling her not to say anything. "Fine, *St. Elmo's Fire* first."

"Yay! I do love that one." Hadley admits.

Ryan squeezes my thigh, and murmurs close to my ear, "You're gonna need to spill that later, babe."

I nod cautiously, my mind races as I try to come up with an excuse. We may not have a label, but there is no way in hell Anya would be ok with someone else kissing me that isn't Clay.

My eyes flutter open as Ryan sits up quickly like there's a fire under her ass. I groan at the loss of her warmth; I was so comfortable spooning her. With a quick glance around I realize we must have fallen asleep in the middle of *About Last Night*.

Ryan is giggling as she stares down at her phone texting who I can only assume is Greyson. I don't know how I feel about that man yet. After several moments her phone rings just as muffled moans sound from Hadley and Connor's room. *Of course they would be fucking right now.*

"Why?" She giggles.

I track Ryan's movements as she paces back and forth.

"Are you worried you have some competition, Daddy?" She's being sassy, ok it's kind of hot. "I fell asleep on the couch with Pickle. She's a snuggler," She explains.

"What's happening?" I sit up, whispering the question. Hearing only one side of a conversation is annoying, I need the tea.

Before she has a chance to give me any information my own phone vibrates with a notification. A new group chat has been created with Clay and Anya. My heart soars with hope.

Clay:

Hey Princess, we figured it would be best to use a group chat. How did you sleep?

Kat:

I slept fine, Ry and I fell asleep on the couch...d on't beat around the bush. Tell me.

Anya:

You're so bossy, Pickle.

I roll my eyes at her response. She's not wrong, but also – what happened.

Kat:

The suspense is killing me. Please!

Clay:

If this is something you want, we're in.

Kat:

Did you two have sex?

Anya:

Yes.

It's not normal that I'm excited about that tidbit of information, is it?

No Princess, probably not. But it's part of why we love you.

Can we back up a bit though, who is Ry and why were you sleeping with them?

I giggle as I imagine her spiraling unnecessarily.

Never mind, Clay explained. Stop laughing at me, Kat.

You make it too easy, Bunny.

We're leaving soon for the appointment. I can't wait to show you what I decided on.

Hadley's tattoos came out beautifully. The intricate linework is absolutely stunning. When she's done and cleaned up, Ryan turns to me expectantly. I had chatted privately with Greyson a few days ago about potential ideas. When I asked that he keep it between us because I'm not ready to share it with the girls, he was more understanding than I probably deserve considering how much shit I've given him about Ryan.

"Do you guys mind if I do this alone? I'll show you eventually I'm just..." I pause as I try to stop the tears from coming. "I need some time before I can share this specific piece of me. Ok?"

"Sure, we'll just wait out here?" Hadley responds, though it comes out more as a question than a statement. I offer a weak smile unsure what else I can say.

Once they're gone, Greyson closes the door behind them and turns to me.

"So, it's that one then, huh?" He grins at me. "I can't wait to meet them."

"Shut up," I groan. "They're going to be so pissed. They've never met Anya, but they hate her for what happened in college."

"Wait, Anya? Brown and pink hair? Cute? Nice figure?" He shoots question after question.

"Um, yea? How do you know her?" I cock a brow at him.

He moves around the room as he gets everything set up for my design. He meticulously places ink caps in a line as he fills them with the colors we agreed on for this option. Once he has the needles out and ready to go, he motions for me to pull my pants down.

"You know, just because I'm taking my pants off for you, doesn't mean I'm going to let that question go." I say to him as I pop the button to my jeans open and slide them down over my hips.

"I may have hit on her when I was at a bar a few weeks ago." He says as he preps my skin. "She called me out on my bullshit, immediately able to tell that I have feelings for Ry without even seeing us together."

I giggle. "Yea, that sounds like her.

"She also told me she was involved; I didn't bother asking for more because – well, Ryan." He shrugs as he starts the tattoo.

A while later, I feel more comfortable with this man for one of my best friends than I was when I first walked in here. He wipes off the excess ink and blood before he points to a mirror. I stand and take a deep breath before I take a look at his handiwork

A dark vine colored in shades of red and brown starts at my hip. The thorn covered stem curves around the contours of my body until it ultimately turns into everything that we are in a space where only they will ever see. Everything that we represent, a symbol of the three of us, a heart with an infinity symbol with beautiful cherry blossoms in various stages of their life to show our new beginning, as the three of us become one.

Chapter Twenty

Kat is so invested in this working that she gave me as much insight as she could before leaving this afternoon. Using a recipe that Anya used to be obsessed with consisting of barbecue chicken along with mac and cheese, the meal is ready to serve at Kat's insistence. Why am I nervous? No matter what happens, I still have my girl.

A soft knock sounds on the front door, I round the counter of the kitchen and head toward the sound. I open the door to see Anya, this time she looks completely different. Whether it's my desire to make Kat happy or the fact that she is looking at me as if I am the balm to her soul, I have no idea.

Anya's beautiful curves are wrapped by a poor excuse of a dress that just covers her ass with an obnoxiously low square neckline that barely conceals her nipples. The blue fabric really makes her eyes pop and damn, my cock twitches in my jeans at the sight of her.

Well, shit. It's gonna be a long night.

"Hey," Anya smiles shyly and walks past me into the apartment.

"Hey, yourself." I wink at her. "You in that dress is the epitome of perfection. You're gorgeous."

We stare at each other for a few moments in silence before she cracks.

"This is weird, right?" She chews her lip which only makes me wonder what she tastes like first-hand.

"Sorry, what?" Unable to hide my distraction she giggles.

"This," she waves a hand gesturing between us. "It's weird. Right?"

I cock a brow, confused. I did read the conversation with her and Kat. She did say she was down for this.

"It's just," Anya lets out a frustrated sigh. "I know you don't like me. If you're just doing this for Kat, we can keep doing what we've been doing."

An amused chuckle escapes which only seems to piss her off. I reach for her wrist and spin her back toward me. Once her body is pressed against mine, I grip the nape of her neck. As soon as her gaze is on me, my mouth crashes against hers. I kiss the ever-loving shit out of her until she melts into me. A soft whimper leaves her as our kiss molds into a mixture of tongue and teeth. Obviously, we've been needing this for the past few weeks. It takes a few moments before we come up for air.

"Fuck, that was. Ok – so you're not just here for her." She mewls.

"No, I'm here for you too, Little Rabbit." My lips twitch as she rolls her eyes at the pet name.

"Ugh! Not you too." She groans.

I press a soft kiss against her lips again as I release her from my grip. "Come on."

After leading Anya to the roof where I have a table set up with fairy lights for ambiance, of course, I pour a glass of wine for her before heading back down to grab our food. The moment I place her plate in front of her, she begins to giggle. I furrow my brow in confusion. "It's just, I can't believe she remembered this. The first time she tried to make this, she set a pan on fire. We had to call the fire department." Anya's laugh is infectious as she reminisces about a time with Kat when I didn't know either of them.

"So, she has a habit of causing fires in kitchens?" I tease as I remember the first time we messed around.

"Basically," Anya smirks.

The evening goes on with more small talk, comfortable silence, and in depth conversations. Really everything you could hope for on a first date. Once we're both done eating, I pull out a game.

"What is this?" She asks as she eyes my hands shuffling the cards.

"Since we're in a unique situation, my normal first date plans aren't an option. Don't worry, you'll get a re-do because I have the perfect idea for you." I grin at her. "But I wanted to do something a little competitive. They're icebreaker questions – if you don't answer, you drink." I shrug as I hand her the deck to pull from the top.

She bites her lip seductively which does nothing to keep my already aching dick from throbbing in my pants. Anya pulls a card and looks at it briefly before reading it aloud.

"What was your first impression of me?" She keeps her eyes on me.

"Seriously? That's the first question?" I chortle at the memory.

"Well, now I definitely need to know." Anya's eyes go wide with concern.

"I thought that you were sexy as hell and that Kat would be smitten if she saw you." I choke out through fits of laughter.

Anya grins at me like she just won the lottery. "Really?"

"Yes, Little Rabbit." I wink at her and grab the next card.

"What is the last thing you masturbated to?" I read the card to her without giving myself time to register the question.

Anya's cheeks tinge pink as she contemplates her next move. She bites her lip, something I notice she does a lot when she's nervous.

"The way you look at me when you cum inside Kat while she's eating me." Anya's voice is barely above a whisper. "The memory of that is seared in my permanent spank bank."

"Oh, Little Rabbit. I will happily relive that moment with the two of you as often as you like." My grin is wicked.

The next card she picks makes her lips turn into a Cheshire grin. *Oh shit.* "What is your hottest sexual fantasy?" Her voice is strong when she asks the question.

God damnit, shit. I haven't even had this conversation with Kat. Fuck, here goes.

"I'd like Kat to use her strap on with me while you suck my cock." I admit.

A soft moan leaves Anya when I finish speaking. Understandably, she wasn't expecting that. I watch her nervously as I wait for a strong reaction.

"Yes, please. Sign me up for that." She licks her lips as her eyes rake down my chest. A gleam in her eye tells me she's up to something. I don't know her well enough to know what to expect yet. When she rises to her feet and saunters around the table to where I sit, I go still. She drops to her knees before me and quickly works to free my cock.

"An, you don't need to -," my words end in a long loud groan as she takes the crown into her mouth and sucks gently around the head. Her hands rest gently on my legs as I palm her cheek. She takes more and more of me with each bob of her head, my length disappearing further down her throat. A sharp gasp escapes when I feel her hollow her cheeks half a second before she takes me deeper. "Fuccckk!"

I can't help but compare her to Kat, which makes me feel instantly guilty. Anya is sweet and fun, but Kat is my heart. Guilt begins to overwhelm me; suddenly the thoughts that are plaguing me vanish as Anya sucks my soul straight out of my cock.

"Jesus Christ, Little Rabbit." I groan, my hands wrap around her luscious locks as I thrust into her throat. She gags around me and I try to ease out, but her nails dig into my thighs. She doesn't want me to go easy on her. Oh fuck, she's going to kill me. My balls tighten and tingles start at the base of my spine. Anya dips her hand into my pants and tugs firmly on my sack. *Fuck me.* "Babygirl, I'm gonna come." I warn her, but she just keeps moving. Seconds later my cock swells as hot ropes of come flood her throat. My body is on cloud nine as the high of my release flows through me. Anya swallows with no complaint, a smug grin planted on her face when she stands in front of me.

My arms wrap around her, and I pull her in for a kiss. Our tongues tangle in a heated exchange. She grins against my lips just before she jumps into my arms and wraps her legs around my waist. We separate just long enough for her to tell me what she wants.

"I need you to fuck me. I've been dying to feel you stretch my pussy since the first time I saw you enter Kat." She admits with a giddiness I didn't expect.

"Jesus, the two of you are going to be the death of me." I chuckle and stand, keeping her in my arms.

My eyes flutter open from a deep sleep to see Anya watching me sleep. I grin before I roll over and pin her to the bed. My lips find hers greeting her with a deep kiss. She whimpers against my lips before pushing me away.

"Not yet, Magic Mike." She giggles as she says the nickname.

"Hell, that's gonna stick, isn't it?" I groan.

"Probably," she winks. "I think we need to tell her."

My brow furrows with confusion. "Yea, that's been the plan."

Anya rolls her eyes at me and sits up; the sheet falls around her waist. Her bare tits on full display does nothing to help the already noticeable morning wood tenting the sheets.

"Obviously, I just mean we should tell her now." She sighs, "I know she wanted this, but it feels like we're hiding something from her if we don't tell her right now."

"You're overthinking, Little Rabbit. But fine." I groan and grab my phone from the night stand.

"Start a group chat. We need to make sure we're all on the same page." She says quietly.

I turn back to Anya and press a soft kiss against her lips. "This was her idea. Why are you so nervous? She's going to be thrilled."

"I don't know, I've never done anything like this before. I haven't dated in years and then, sharing each other? I'm just – I don't know, I'm freaking out." She rambles on.

"Breathe, Rabbit. It's going to be ok. We've never done anything like this either. We're going to figure it out together." I smile and type out a message. Her phone dings as soon as I press send. "There, now we wait for a response."

Chapter Twenty-One

Anya

Kat hadn't messaged either of us while she was at the tattoo shop. It shouldn't have me worried since we never used to be in constant contact, yet my stomach is in knots. Clay's arms are wrapped snugly around my middle as we lay on the couch. He's very into his current binge of True Blood. Whether it's for Anna Paquin or he's just that interested in vampires, I"m not sure. I guess all things considered, I'm glad he's watching this.

Bill and Eric are fighting again when the door to the back entrance opens slowly, Kat strolls in with no care in the world. Only to stop suddenly when she sees the two of us cuddled up together. *Shit, I knew this was too good to be true.* I struggle and try to move from Clay's grip.

"Breathe Little Rabbit," he chuckles against my neck before pressing a feather-light kiss to my exposed skin.

"Oh my god! It's really happening!" Kat squeals as she bounds over to us. She climbs onto the couch with her thighs stretched wide as she straddles both Clay and my legs.

She grips my chin, her lips crash against my mouth in a molten kiss. I whine as she pulls away to share a moment with Clay. Her tits are directly in front of my face as she kisses him. With a wicked chuckle I nip her pebbled peak through the thin shirt. She moans softly and grips my hair to pull me away from her as she sits up.

"Not yet." She scolds me teasingly. "Tell me everything about last night." She has an infectious smile on her face.

I giggle and gently adjust her so that we're not in such an intimate position while I tell her about how I fucked her boyfriend. Or I guess our boyfriend now. Once she's seated on the coffee table in front of us, I go into everything that happened last night. Kat grows bored quickly and rolls her eyes.

"Yea, I'm glad that y'all get along but I want the dirty details." She waggles her eyebrows suggestively.

I choke on a laugh as Clay shakes his head.

"What you're asking is how we fucked?" Clay's bluntness surprises me even though it shouldn't.

"Exactly, did you do that thing with your tongue?" She asks Clay before directing her gaze to me, her cheeks tinge the prettiest shade of pink. "Did you like it?"

"Whoa, Princess." Clay chortles.

"What? I've been dying to know." She shrugs as if it should be obvious that this line of questioning was coming. She leans forward like a toddler at story time.

I've been begging him to fuck me for I don't know how long. His brilliantly talented tongue swirls tight circles around the sensitive bundle of nerves. I squirm as yet another orgasm builds. Every nerve ending in my body is like a live wire ready to blow.

"Fuck! Clay! Yes!" I cry out, the pleasure is too great. My back arches off the bed as my crescendo climbs to new heights. As soon as I collapse back onto the mattress, I feel his mouth trailing soft kisses up my stomach. It's not until his lips collide with mine does he finally give me what I've been begging for.

It's been so long since I've been with a man, let alone one that cares about my pleasure enough to make sure I'm sated before he takes what he needs. Of course, that's just how Clay would operate.

"You ok, Little Rabbit?" He's being so gentle, it's endearing.

"I'll be much better when you're inside me, Magic Mike." I tease as I raise my head to kiss him.

The moment our lips connect, I feel Clay slowly start to slide himself inside me. I close my eyes as soon as I feel just how big he is. Fuck, this was a bad idea. I gasp when I feel his thumb on my clit.

"Come on, Babygirl. Stretch for me." He grins as he eases himself in a bit more.

A wicked grin spreads across my face when he's finally fully seated. He begins to slowly pump in and out. I need more.

"Clay," I cry out through a moan. "Fuck me like I'm your whore." I beg, before I bury my face into his neck. Soft nips and kisses at the sensitive skin aren't enough to set him off the way I want. I groan loudly and thrust my hips up to meet his. His hand wraps tightly around my neck which just turns me on even more. My cunt squeezes his thick rod as the thrusts deep inside me.

"Fuck, Rabbit!" He growls and finally gives me what I've been begging for. Without warning he pulls out and flips me onto my stomach. Clay's hands are on my hips as he pulls me back onto my knees. Once my ass is in the air he slides home again. His fingertips dig deep into my skin. I can already feel bruises forming from his tight grip. My pussy weeps around his cock as he nails me to the bed. My legs begin to tremble as another climax builds.

"Clay!" I whimper just as one hand releases my hip and finds my clit. He pinches the sensitive bundle of nerves, sending me over the edge one more time.

"That's it, Little Rabbit. Let me have it." He groans, I feel his cock swell inside me just before he finds his own release.

Kat whimpers and squeezes her legs together as we finish relaying the details of Clay and my time together.

"I can't wait to see that." She's breathing heavily.

"In due time, Pickle." My lips twitch into a promising smile before I press a quick kiss to her forehead. "I think we need to make everything clear for all of us though. Especially since none of us have done this before." I try to act unbothered by any of this even though my anxiety is still running rampant.

"Ok, what do you want to discuss?" Kat asks, her eyes locked on me.

"I don't want to share either of you with anyone else." I admit quickly.

"I second that." Clay chimes in.

Kat glances between the two of us before speaking.

"That's easy. I don't want anyone other than the two of you." Kat grins. "What else?" She asks.

"How do we handle telling people our status?" I glance between Clay and Kat, "Everyone already knows the two of you are together but what about me?"

"Listen, I don't give a fuck what people think. If y'all want to hire a sky writer, let me know. If you want to keep it between us that's fine too." Clay's answer makes me snort.

"A sky writer? Really?" My lips twist as I try to fight back a laugh. "I don't mind if we tell everyone or wait, Kat?"

Kat doesn't speak for several minutes, tears well in her beautiful blue eyes. Before I can ask what's wrong she stands and begins to pace the length of the living room.

"I want to tell everyone, but we can't, not yet. She. I." She shakes her head as she continues to panic. "We, not yet. We can't. I'm sorry." The tears are streaming down her cheeks now.

"Hey, Princess. It's ok. We can wait to tell everyone." Clay stands and pulls her into a tight hug. "For what it's worth, I think she'll be more understanding than you're giving her credit for."

I cock a brow not exactly sure what could be causing this kind of reaction until Clay mouths "Hadley" to me. It all clicks into place. Welp, I guess it's just going to be the three of us for a while. Maybe that's for the best.

Chapter Twenty-Two

As happy as I am, why do I feel like I'm on a roller coaster? My stomach is about to drop no matter what I do. Clay just wants us both to be happy. Anya doesn't care if we go public as long as she has the two of us.

A loud groan escapes. I know what my problem is, but I'm afraid to do anything about it. I grab my phone as I head down to my car.

Any chance I can come by? I need to talk.

My phone rings with an unknown caller as soon as I press send. I quickly press ignore since anyone I know would already be stored. A response from Alannah comes in quick.

You are always welcome to come over.

Thanks babe. I'm walking to my car now.

Alannah isn't too far from Connor's. I mean it kind of makes sense, he is her brother. However today I'm anxious at the possibility that Hadley could see my car here when I haven't talked to her since she dropped me off after the tattoo. I take in the suburban streets as I drive. My heart is pounding chaotically in my chest as I wait to see my friend.

The front door swings open to a red-haired beauty who only slightly resembles Connor. "What's the story with ya, love!" She takes me in and gasps. "What the feckin' hell happened?" Her Irish accent comes out so much stronger with some words. It's so endearing.

"Can I come in?" I ask hesitantly.

"Of course, of course!" She steps to the side to allow me in.

Her son Sean is sitting in the living room with his boyfriend watching old episodes of Will and Grace. I can't help but smirk at the sight before me. Alannah loops an arm around mine and pulls me into the kitchen.

"What happened?" She asks again.

"I need this to stay between us. I'm not ready for Hadley to know." I force out.

"Ok? Tell me what's going on?" She asks warily.

"Do you remember how I mentioned my girlfriend from college?" I ask as nonchalantly as I can muster. She nods, a question in her eyes. "Well, she's kind of back in the picture. But before you yell at me. This was Clay's idea. Well, not initially, she kind of came back by accident, but then when he realized who she was he insisted I give her a chance." I rush out so fast I would make Lorelai Gilmore proud.

"Ok. So, he told you to leave him for her?" She asks dumbfounded.

"No, they've been sharing me..." I pause and take in her shocked expression. "I asked them to see if they had chemistry since I wasn't going to be home last night to be in the way and well. They did, so now we're all together. Or well, we will be when I get home."

"Ahh, I see." She takes a deep breath before she continues. "And you're afraid to tell Hadley because of how she and Connor met?"

I nod with tears in my eyes, I don't bother hiding them this time.

"The thing is, I am happy. It may not be conventional, but I feel whole when the three of us are together." My confession startles even myself.

"I'm not going to tell her, but I think it's something you need to be honest about." Alannah shrugs. "You aren't Andy. No one forced this on any of you."

"You're right." I sigh, "Honestly, I'm terrified it's going to trigger her."

"She's stronger than that." Alannah rolls her eyes at me. "When you're ready to tell her, let me know and I can let Connor know so he is prepared and can be watching in case something changes."

"Do you think she'll hate me?" Unable to hide the emotion in my voice as I ask the question that has been plaguing my mind since I realized this wasn't going to be a short-term situation no matter how last night went.

"I think she may need some time to process, but Hadley adores you. She'll never abandon you or your friendship." Alannah pulls me into a sweet embrace.

The sky is a bright array of colors as I pull up to Karma. I smile to myself as I sit in the car watching the sun slowly set. Before it can disappear into the night, I walk in through the front door. Ava is chatting with a member; I see Clay leaning against a weight rack as he watches a regular do bicep curls. With a wicked grin plastered across my face, I saunter toward him. His eyes brighten when he sees me walk toward him.

"Hey, beautiful," Clay's smooth voice sends a rush of heat to my core. I close the distance between us and my mouth crashes against his. His arms immediately mold to my figure and hold on to me, I melt into him as the passion we share fuses us together by our lips. I whimper softly into the erotic exchange. His tongue teases me as we get lost in one another. After a few moments he pulls away, separating the two of us. A frustrated whine leaves my lips which makes him chuckle. "Well, hello. What happened at Alannah's?" He asks.

"I wasn't done kissing you." I pout. The reaction only seems to entertain him even more. "She helped ease my mind. Well, kind of." I shrug.

"Why would your mind not be at ease? We all want this, don't we?" He asks, confusion clear on his face.

"No, no! I'm thrilled with the three of us. It's the telling..." I glance around the room to make sure no one is around who knows any of us only to realize the member who was working out next to us is on the treadmill with a knowing smirk on his face. My cheeks flush but when I'm sure we're clear I finish my thought. "It's the telling Hadley that I'm stressed about. Because of what she went through with Andy."

"Princess, this is nothing like that." Clay smirks at me like I'm ridiculous.

"Maybe not, but I'm nervous at how she's going to respond." I let out a defeated sigh. "We'll find out when I decide to tell her."

We stand there for several minutes, just enjoying the closeness.

"Where is my daughter," I hear a familiar venomous voice from behind me. Clay's body goes rigid. His arms tense around me and I can feel the fury radiating off of him. I gently place my hand on his chest and free myself enough to confirm the voice belongs to. As soon as I see his face, even if he's aged over the years since I last saw him, I know, it's him. "Daddy?"

Chapter Twenty-Three

My blood is boiling under my skin as Kat's father steps closer to us. I squeeze her tighter against me to shield from the onslaught of chaos that is bound to come along with this shithead.

After only seeing pictures years ago not long after we met, the knowledge of how her parents treated her seared their images in my brain the moment she told me who they were. I vowed to not allow them near her again. He looks much the same, save for some wrinkles around his eyes. The man standing before us is dressed like the pompous ass I know he truly is. A sweater vest over a white button up dress shirt and dress pants completes the look of the arrogant man he is.

How the hell did my woman come from that vile being?

"Daddy?" She asks in a demure tone I've never heard her use before.

Silence stretches for what feels like ages before anyone talks again. Of course, it's the person who would have me in need of bail money that starts talking first.

"Where is my daughter, you filthy whore!" He snarls at me.

Without any further thought, I lift Kat into my arms and move her behind me. My fists ball at my sides as I take a step closer to Mr. Kensington. My face must clearly show my anger because he stumbles back a step.

"I don't give a flying fuck who the fuck you are, you will not speak to Kat that way." I say as calmly as my emotions will allow. Spoiler – it comes out somewhere between a growl and a snarl.

Unfortunately, the asshole doesn't leave. He cranes his neck to see Kat who is clinging to my back. He scoffs at her before he continues to speak.

"We found her second phone, how long have you been in contact?" He begins to rapidly fire questions at Kat. "How many times has she been here? What kind of lies did you fill her head with?"

Before I can respond Kat finds her voice and replies. Just not how he was expecting.

"I've been fine since you disowned me, Daddy. Thanks for asking." Kat replies cooly. "I'm so glad you stopped by to see how I've been doing. Things were touch and go for a while if I'm honest."

My mask falters for just a moment as I hear her speak to him like he is genuinely here for her. I glance over my shoulder to see her standing tall. She's ready to take on the world. My heart beats full of pride at just how far she's come.

"I don't give a rat's ass, Katrina." The way she flinches tells me just how deep that response cuts. "Though, I'm glad to see you're fucking a man now, the way it's supposed to be."

My control snaps and I lunge for him, my fists grip the collar of his shirt, and I pull him to my face. The way my lips twist into a wicked grin seems to bring him enough fear that his eyes widen.

"Actually, she's fucking a man and a woman. How does that make you feel, you, worthless twat waffle." I say through gritted teeth. His eyes flash with abject horror which pleases me. "You should be ashamed of yourself, even showing your face here. You abandoned your daughter a decade ago. There's nothing for you here, not now. Not ever, dickhead." I drop the older man to the ground and shove him backward until he's only a few steps from the door.

"You, you're all disgusting!" He shouts back at us.

Kat's expression shows no emotion which is just a tad alarming. She steps forward and takes my hand as she speaks to her father.

"If you haven't figured it out, yet. We're not telling you shit." She steps into her dad's space as she continues. "If you ever come near me again, I will make sure everyone knows exactly what you made her hide."

"You don't frighten me, child." He scoffs. "I'll get the information from you one way or another. Or else."

Without another word he slinks out of the front door. Kat turns to me and buries her face in my chest. I wrap my arms tightly around her as we both come to terms with what just happened. A few moments later I feel a hand gently tap my shoulder. I turn my face to see Ava.

"Hey, guys. I got everyone to leave out the back when I realized who that was." She smiles weakly before turning her attention to Kat. "I didn't think anyone needed to know your business."

"Thank you, Ava," Kat's expression is full of warmth as she releases me and engulfs Ava in a hug.

The two of them separate after a minute and Ava tells us she's locking up early so we can decompress. *I really need to give that girl a raise.* With a nod, I turn to Kat, and I lace my fingers with hers and lead her up to our place.

The moment we step through the threshold she buries her face into my chest once again and lets out an earth-shattering scream that tears through my soul. I hold her tight doing what I can to comfort her after what was an infuriating interaction for me. I can't begin to imagine the emotions she's processing.

Unsure how much time has passed; I lift her into my arms and carry Kat to the couch where I continue to hold her. Part of me wants to call Anya and ask her to come over, but I don't want to overwhelm her either. Fucking hell.

"Princess." I whisper into her hair as she continues to cling onto me.

"Yeah?" Her voice cracks through the short word.

Feeling helpless, I ask. "What do you need? What can I do?"

It takes a while before she answers me. Her answer surprisingly gives me comfort knowing that she's not shutting down or shutting anyone out.

"I need to talk to Auggie." She breathes.

Without hesitation I lift her enough to pull her phone from her back pocket where she always shoves it. Once it's in her hand she taps furiously on the screen. When she's done, she drops the phone to her lap and stares up at me, her eyes full of adoration.

Chapter Twenty-Four

The emotions slam into me, like a ferocious tsunami would wreck a quiet beach with its destruction. I'm unable to concentrate on myself until I talk to my brother. I don't understand why Penny would leave without saying goodbye. A frantic scream leaves me when I realize just how long it's been since I've spoken to her. I've been so consumed by my own life I haven't bothered to reach out to her since the day Anya popped back into my life. Anger must radiate from me when I send a text to Auggie who doesn't bother responding.

"Kat, baby. I'm here. What do you need?" Clay's voice comes out rougher than usual. The way he spoke to my father must have strained his usual smoothness. I can sense his worry which only sends me even deeper into a tailspin of emotion.

My eyes land on his with a pleading gaze, I'm unable to articulate my needs as everything inside me is a maze of chaos. The anxiety I feel rolling through has me on my feet. Time stands still as I spiral; my surroundings fade into a darkness. I can't hear Clay's voice anymore, only my own thoughts. Every worst-case scenario plays out in my mind's eye as I pace back and forth the length of the living room. Why would she vanish without telling me? Why didn't I tell her about Anya? No, I know the answer to that last one. As much as I love having her back in my life, I've been terrified of them finding out even if I believe she's trying to get away from them.

Suddenly, a set of small but strong hands land on my shoulders, her sweet scent penetrates my senses as her hands travel to my neck and finally cup my cheeks. I blink rapidly to bring everything back into focus to find Anya standing before me. Her eyes are full of tears. She's been crying. It's enough to snap me back to reality and I wrap her tightly in an embrace.

"Bunny." I cry into her neck.

"I know Pick, I know." Neither of us move for a while.

I can sense Clay hovering near us, and I reach out to him. He wraps himself around both of us in a beat. For a brief moment I feel peace in the all-encompassing madness that is working its way into our world.

"Kat," Anya whispers as she and Clay pull away and guide me back to the couch. "I don't know everything that was said today, but I know what you've told me in the past. What was said tonight doesn't matter because you are a remarkable woman who is loved, not just by the two of us, but by anyone who knows you. Your parents don't know you anymore. Hell, even if they did, their opinion isn't valid here." She tucks a stray lock of hair behind my ear.

"I know." I sniff back tears. "Knowing their opinion hasn't changed and they're still as poisonous as ever shouldn't be a surprise." I shrug and let out a long-drawn-out sigh. "My sadness and fear has more to do with Penny than it has to do with myself."

Clay cocks a brow at me, silently calling me out on my bullshit.

"Ok fine, yes. I'm hurt and upset. Of course I am, he's my dad for Christ's sake!" I shout louder than I intend.

"Baby, it's going to be ok. We're going to figure this out, none of it is your fault." Anya's gentle voice calms me. "Penny has been planning to leave right? Maybe it just needed to be an expedited escape. Based on what she's told you, it's possible, don't you think? She may have just left with Deke sooner than anticipated."

Her words turn over in my brain and the turmoil in my mind quiets just long enough to realize my phone is ringing. I dart between the two of them to grab the device. I see my brother's smiling face on the screen as his contact image takes up the screen. After swiping the green button to answer I bring the phone to my ear.

"Auggie! Where is she? Do you know where she is?" I rush out question after question not allowing him to respond immediately.

"KitKat," he sighs. "Breathe, she's fine and with Deke."

I let out a sigh of relief before I start in on the interrogation.

"Where the hell is she?" I ask, "Dad showed up at Karma this afternoon." After letting that fact settle on him, I start again, "You had me fucking ambushed, why?" I sob into the phone.

"Fuck, that piece of shit. I'm sorry Kat, we never thought they'd track you down." Auggie, always the protective big brother snarls. "I'll take care of this. They won't contact you again."

"Back up. Why won't you tell me where she is?" My anxiety is at full force.

"It's just safer right now. As soon as we can tell you, we will." He replies gingerly. I hear a commotion in the background, a muffled grunt sounds before another voice comes on the line.

"Hey Kat? It's Poc – Chloe." She stumbles over her name. "I promise you she is safe; she is where no harm will come to her. My sister was taken captive when we were kids so I'm telling you everything I can, so you don't go through what I did. Not knowing is absolutely awful, but I need you to trust us right now. Alright?"

"Can I talk to her?" I ask as tears rush down my cheeks.

Chloe's silence speaks volumes before she even says a word. "Here's the thing, to keep everyone safe, she's not with us. She's with Deke, and I don't know if you've seen the man, but no one in their right mind would go up against him."

"I've seen him, he makes the Incredible Hulk look like a Good Luck Troll doll." Unable to hold back a snort, I continue. "Did they find –" But I don't get to finish my question, Chloe cuts me off.

"We can't share any details. She'll call you as soon as she can. Ok?" Chloe's response is colder than she was a few minutes ago.

"Yea, thanks, Chloe." I breathe as the line goes dead.

Chapter Twenty-Five

Anya

A mixture of emotion is still radiating from Kat when she puts her phone down on the table. She rolls her shoulders back and stands tall before she turns to Clay. Her expression changes to something heated and needy as she wanders over to him. I can see from where I'm standing that she's kissing the life out of him. He stumbles backward, unprepared for the fierceness in her lips.

My lips twitch into a grin as I watch the show before me. Fuck, I love to watch them together. By the time Kat pulls away, Clay is panting. I notice him adjusting his dick in his pants just as she closes the distance to where I stand. Her mouth is on mine in an instant, a kiss filled with so much passion and desire, my knees tremble underneath me. Her tongue coaxes my lips to part as she slips inside and kisses the shit out of me. Kat's arms snake around my waist to keep me on my feet when she pulls away several moments later.

"Jesus Christ, Kat." Clay groans, his hand still wrapped tightly around his bulge.

She glances at him and then turns to make eye contact with me.

"I need to see the two of you now." Kat holds her hand out for me to take. Once my fingers are laced with her she leads me to the bedroom.

Suddenly I'm feeling shy as hell. Sure, I've gotten Kat off while she's been with him, or she's gone down on me while he fucks her. But this is the first time I'm the star of the show, so to speak. Before I can speak, I turn around to see Clay leaning in the doorway. Jesus, why is that hot?

His beautiful golden-brown gaze takes me in as he crosses the room in the most sensual stroll I've ever seen. Strong, calloused hands are on me in a flash. Clay's intense stare as he drags my shirt up over my head has my clit throbbing. He caresses my skin with every move he makes, which has me whimpering for more.

"Clay," I plead.

"I got you, Little Rabbit." He smirks just before his lips are on mine. I feel his hands on my bare ass as he helps me shimmy out of my leggings. My pulse hammers so hard I can hear the whoosh whoosh whoosh whoosh of blood pumping in my veins. The moment my legs are free from the tight spandex, Clay lifts me into his arms just to lay me gently on the bed. A wicked grin spreads across his face just before he disappears from my view.

Seconds later, his shirt is thrown onto the mattress, somewhere in my peripheral and his tongue delves between my folds. The moan that escapes me sounds feral. It only urges Clay on. He skillfully swipes and swirls around the sensitive bundle of nerves as I writhe beneath him. I hear a heady whimper which pulls my attention to Kat who is clenching her thighs as she sits on a chair in the corner watching. Clay slides a finger inside me at the same moment. Knowing how much seeing us together is affecting her sends me over the edge. My pussy clamps down on his finger as he sucks my clit hard.

"Fuck! Yes!" I sob as I ride out my release.

"God, An. You're gorgeous when you come on his tongue." I hear Kat's whispered commentary as I come down from my orgasmic high. "I can't wait to see your reaction to his cock spreading you open."

My lips twitch into a knowing grin just as I feel the tip of Clay's generous cock at my entrance. "Fuck me, Magic Mike."

The smirk he flashes back at me sends a new rush of heat between my thighs, just in time for him to thrust in. My nerve endings are still on high alert after the orgasm he just gave me that it doesn't take long before his movements have me nearing the edge. I cry out as another orgasm hits and my body spasms with intensity.. My eyes close and my head pushes back into the bed without my permission in response.

"FUCK!" Clay growls as my cunt tightens so hard around him, he can't move. The moment my body relaxes I feel him pull out, and a tongue swipes the length of my pussy which only makes my body spasm once more. Kat climbs up my body and presses a soft kiss against my lips.

"You look like you could use a minute?" She asks with a wide grin spread across her gorgeous face.

"Yes please." I pant. My eyes flutter open when I realize I feel her bare skin. When the hell did that happen?

I shuffle back onto the bed and lean against the headboard while I watch them. Clay pulls Kat in for a kiss to end all kisses. The love they share is so breathtaking. I can't help the pang of jealousy. I know I have that kind of love with her. One day, I hope I have it with him as well.

In the blink of an eye, she's laying on her back, her head hanging off the edge of the bed. Unable to look away, I take in the scene before me. Clay stands before her and taps her lips with his cock. *Oh my god.* I can see as she opens her mouth, and he slides in. He's gentle at first while her hands are on her tits, the second she pinches her nipple is apparently a sign she wants more. He thrusts once inside her mouth harder than before and she moans loudly around him. Fuck, it's muffled, but god damnit is it sexy as hell.

Kat's hands travel down her toned stomach to her pussy. She dips a finger in and swirls her arousal over her clit and starts to play with herself as he holds her face and continues the assault on her throat. It lasts for only a few minutes before he pulls out and motions for her to spin toward him. She rolls onto her stomach and climbs to her knees in front of him. They share another kiss and before he can make any motion, she grips his throat and tells him to lay down.

"Holy shit, Kat." I moan and clench my legs together in need of some sort of friction to calm myself. I'm so ready for another orgasm, it's hard to concentrate. My own hand travels unwittingly between my thighs. I groan when my fingers enter my tight cunt as I begin to fuck myself while I watch them.

Clay chuckles darkly but does as he's told. Once he's on his back, Kat straddles him and slides him inside with ease. *Oh god.* She moans softly and allows herself to adjust for a moment.

"Bunny?" She calls my name like it's not the first time she's tried to get my attention. *Oops.*

"Yea? Sorry." I stop all movements to give her my undivided attention.

"You're going to ride his face while I ride his cock. I want the three of us to come together." She grins as she bounces on Clay's cock. He groans and reaches for me.

I'm unable to protest since his hands wrap around my thighs and lift me onto his face, my front to Kat's. I cry out and double over, my hands dart out and grip onto Kat's shoulders. When Clay's tongue first starts its exploration as he spears his tongue inside me while his finger presses against my tight asshole.

Kat giggles when she realizes what he's done and swats his chest.

"Unless you're close, don't do that! I want to see her come on your tongue while I'm on your cock." She says with a gleam in her eye as she drops back down. His moan in response has me crying out, the vibration nearly sending me over the edge.

"Jesus, I'm not going to last if you keep doing that to him." I cry out as I grind against Clay's tongue.

She leans down as she ungulates her hips and sucks my nipple into her mouth. I arch my back into her, she's sucking so hard I nearly see stars. Clay grips my hips and holds me still. Kat releases my nipple with an audible pop and I can feel the orgasm building. I reach forward and rub tight circles around her clit and she becomes erratic with how she is taking Clay.

I feel his tongue spear inside me again as he slides a finger into my tight ass sending me over the edge, at the same time he thrusts up into Kat who is falling over the edge with me. The room is filled with a chorus of pleasure filled sounds as we give Kat exactly what she needed from us.

Chapter Twenty-Six

A date, we've needed a date for the three of us since we started this new chapter together. Knowing my hang ups about telling my friends, Clay decided on a brunch date in the city. I've been getting ready for the last thirty minutes. My hair is hanging in loose waves over my shoulders, and I've done a full face of makeup. I must say, I look flawless. After much deliberation – as in I changed my outfit five times – I'm wearing the purple sundress Clay loves with my nude Vans. I release a deep breath and walk out of the bathroom to find Clay leaning against the wall dressed in a dark T-shirt and jeans. *How is he mouthwatering no matter what he wears?*

"You ready, Princess?" He shoots a knowing smirk my way.

"I hate you, yes let's go before we end up in bed." I groan.

He chuckles and slaps my ass as we walk down the stairs. As soon as we get to the car, I climb into the passenger seat, and he pulls me in for a kiss. It's soft yet hot, filled with so much passion and love my panties are ready to combust. When he pulls away a needy whimper passes my lips causing him to chuckle.

"I love you, beautiful." He grins before we make the short drive to Anya's.

She's walking toward the door before either of us can get out to pick her up. The white mini skirt and graphic tee she has paired with a pair of black chucks is sexy as fuck. *Why have I not insisted on taking her out before today?* I swallow hard as she climbs in the back seat.

"Jesus, Little Rabbit." Clay takes the words right out of my mouth.

She giggles and I see her blow him a kiss.

The drive to AllWays Lounge takes longer than I like. The moment I step out of the car and can get my hands on Anya; I push her back against the car and drag her mouth to mine. We kiss like it's the first and last time all at once. It's hot as fuck. When I pull away, she grips my hips and holds me against her for a few seconds longer.

"What was that for?" She pants.

"Thank you for putting up with me and my anxieties. I am excited to have you both on my arm today." I grin up at her before I tangle my fingers with hers.

As soon as I turn around Clay is there with his arm outstretched ready to lead us both in. He has the cockiest of grins on his face which makes me roll my eyes.

"Shut up." I try to be stern in my reaction to his amusement.

"I didn't say a word, just enjoying my girls together." He winks and presses a soft kiss to my temple.

A few hours later we're exiting the drag show, all smiles and laughter. We all had exchanged looks of shock when we saw Mrs. Adams at AllWay's of all places. As we begin making our way back to the car, Clay glances at me with a mischievous grin. Before I know it, he's got Anya over his shoulder and bolting across the street. I shake my head with amusement and step off the sidewalk to see a dark SUV heading right toward them. The vehicle seems to speed up when they're away from me.

Time goes still as I look back at them, they're not going to make it. I don't know if I scream or stay silent. Nothing matters if they're not alright. I take off across the street, passing blurs of people, unable to bring myself to worry about them yet. I crash into the two loves of my life, and the three of us roll through the grass down a short embankment.

A cacophony of screams tear through the normal sounds of traffic as tires screech, followed by a loud crash in the direction we've just come from. I'm not worried about the SUV right now though. I sit up wincing at the stiffness I feel from how I landed. I frantically bounce my gaze between Anya and Clay, checking them over.

"Bunny? Clay, baby!" I cry. Thankfully, Anya begins to stir, only she's moaning in pain and not opening her eyes. I notice a red tint to her hair. *Shit she landed on a rock.* Clay sits bolt upright when he hears her tortured noises. "I'm here, An, we're right here," I correct as Clay grips my hand tightly.

A stranger comes running down the hill to check on us, saying something about an ambulance is on their way. They mention something about a car being missing but there is so much chaos racing through my mind I can't comprehend what they're trying to say.

We've been at the hospital for an hour waiting on results. I had sent a text to Alannah when we were put in separate ambulances freaking out. She responded quickly, so I shouldn't be surprised to see her walking toward me now.

"Lan," I cry and limp toward her, wrapping my arms around her neck.

"Kat, I'm so sorry. What have they said?" She replies with a maternal tone filled with love.

"We're still waiting." I gesture to Anya and Clay who are cuddled together on the hospital bed while I'm on a chair with my hands clasped around Anya's. "Oh my god, Lan. I'm so sorry." I shake my head internally scolding myself as I introduce everyone.

I don't miss the way Anya stiffens when I call her my girlfriend.

"It's a pleasure meeting you both, I just wish it were under better circumstances. We'll have dinner at my place soon, yea?" Her sweet gesture warms my heart.

"I mean, yes that sounds wonderful." Anya says shyly and pries an eye open to find me, "Can we go back to where you said I'm your girlfriend?" Her face lights up.

"Oh, you caught that, huh?" I tease. "Alannah is fully aware of our relationship. All of us." I admit. "She's the only person I knew wouldn't judge, her and her son, because he was there when we talked about it."

"Yes love, you're not a secret." Alannah winks at Anya which makes her blush.

The doctor comes in a few minutes later to inform us I was lucky and got off with a few bruises. Meanwhile Clay has a dislocated shoulder which will be reset before we leave and An has a damn concussion. Once Anya has been scolded and told not to work for at least a week they ask us to hang out a bit longer because the police need to speak with us.

No longer than the doctor steps out do two uniformed officers walk in. The older gentleman who looks like he's seen too much sun speaks first while the younger stands off to the side and observes.

"Good afternoon, I'm officer Paulson and this is Officer Taylor," He gestures to the other man. "I'm sorry to bother you all after what you've been through, but we have some questions."

"It's ok, we'll help however we can." I answer for all three of us.

"Do you know a Leigh Adams?" He asks.

"Uh, yea. She used to be a client at our gym. What does she have to do with this?" I glance at Clay with a terrified expression written across my face.

"She was killed during the incident today. We're trying to determine if she was the target or if you lot were." He pauses briefly, "unfortunately the vehicle drove off before we got there, and we've been unsuccessful in locating it just yet."

Shock clouds the rest of the conversation. I must have stopped answering at some point because eventually Alannah interrupts and steps between us and the officers creating a barrier of one.

"Excuse me, I think they've answered enough at this time. You can speak to them again later if you have more questions. I'm going to take them home."

Chapter Twenty-Seven

Anya

Today is my first day back at work. It's been the longest week of my life. The last time I lay around like this was when I left Kat. At least then I had no drive to do anything else, but now? Now, I'm forced to sit and stare at the wall, generally in the dark, because lights hurt.

Concussions are the worst.

I mean, obviously. No one has ever said they were fun.

Shut up. Great – now I'm having a conversation with myself.

At least it's not out loud.

If I'm honest though, Kat *forcing* me to stay with the two of them has been the highlight of my week. Falling asleep in their bed, the three of us together. It feels right, *we* feel right.

I tug my black leggings over my hips and grab my favorite blouse. Once I'm fully dressed, I rush out of the bedroom to see Kat and Clay kissing against the kitchen counter. A soft gasp passes my lips as I stand and admire the view. Damn, I don't know how I got so fucking lucky.

"Are you gonna to stand there and gawk or are you going to come over here and get involved in some action before you have to leave?" Kat teases from her spot pressed against the countertop.

With an amused smirk twisting my lips I cross the room in a few long strides. I kiss the two of them briefly before pulling away.

"As much as I would love to see what kind of action you're going to get up to while I'm gone. I need to get to work." I reply and peck Kat on the lips once more.

"You're coming back tonight, right?" Kat asks, her voice hopeful.

"Axel asked me to stay at our place tonight so we can catch up," I confess. The way her expression immediately changes. "Pickle, you know I'm not living here, I'll come back in a few days." I say as gently as I can.

She sighs, "I know, it's just been so nice waking up with you in bed with us." Kat forces a smile and waves me off. "Text when you're at work, ok?"

My arms snake around her to keep her close for a few moments before I am out of time.

I'm greeted by a round of applause and cheers when I walk through the door of Capelli. My eyes well up with tears as Axe pulls me into an embrace and murmurs into my ear.

"I've missed you, Louis. That's the longest we've been apart in ages."

"Rick, you visited me every day." I thwack his chest playfully as I pull away. "But I missed you too."

Before I can get too far Lori has me in a hug so tight, J.Lo would be having *Anaconda* flashbacks.

"I know I've seen you, but my god lady. You're never allowed to be in a situation like this ever again. We've missed you." She cries into my shoulder.

It takes a few moments for them both to let me go. Axel has a question etched across his face that he's not asking. My eyes involuntarily roll as I say, "Spit it out. Ask what you want."

"Did they ever find out why that bitch was at the drag bar?" He croaks the question out as though it's been eating him alive.

"Her husband is one of the queens." I reply. Axe and Lori's eyes go so wide I fear they'll pop out of the sockets.

"Get the fuck out." Lori shouts.

A never-ending flow of clients come and go out of my chair throughout the entire day. I feel rejuvenated yet exhausted by the time I sit down. Axe and Lori exchange an amused expression.

"Go home, shower, and change. We'll be there in a bit to have dinner." Axe shakes his head with a knowing smirk.

"I'm fine!" I yawn, causing my cheeks to flush. "Ok, you win. I'll see you guys in a bit."

I grab my phone to see a handful of messages in the group chat.

Pickle:

Have a wonderful day. Call if you need anything!

Magic Mike:

Have a great day, Little Rabbit. Remember to drink lots of water and rest when you can.

Pickle:

Ten bucks says she didn't sit all day.

Magic Mike:

I know better than to place a losing bet.

I chuckle as I cross the yard to our house and reply while I walk upstairs to the shower.

Anya:

I miss you guys too. It was fantastic being back and feeling useful.

Pickle:

But did you sit down before you collapsed after your last client?

Anya:

Are you watching me?

Magic Mike:

And this is why I didn't take that bet.

Pickle:

Doesn't matter, I still win.

I peel my clothes off my body and step into the shower. The molten stream of water relaxes my exhausted muscles. With no desire to be on my feet longer than necessary I wash the day off my skin and turn off the water. I quickly wrap a towel around myself and rush to my room.

After digging through my dresser for several minutes, I find a pair of flannel sweatpants and a tank top. Once I'm dressed, I pad down the stairs where I sit on the couch, curling up against the arm rest. No sooner do I tuck my feet under my bottom does the back door to the house swing open.

"Honey! We're home!" Axel bellows through the house.

"Oh, thank God, I've been helpless here all alone without you." I shoot back sarcastically.

He grips his chest as if he's been shot. "I'm going to take that seriously, otherwise the thought of you not needing me anymore hurts just too much," he quips.

I roll my eyes while smiling brightly, I love my nights with Kat and Clay, but damn. I've missed this man. He's my person, any time I've needed anything since the day we've met he's been the one I've called.

"So, how are things?" Lori prods as she takes a seat next to me on the couch.

Axel sits a pizza on the coffee table and sits cross-legged while taking a slice and watching us.

"Things are fine." I yawn in response while leaning in to grab a piece for myself.

"Louis, spill the tea. How the hell are you walking after the amount of sex you've been having?" Axel rushes out.

Chapter Twenty-Eight

It's been too long since I've spent an evening with my friends. We've all been wrapped up in our own lives and relationships. Our friendship seems to have been pushed to the back burner. Even if I understand it considering I'm juggling two relationships, well actually I guess it's three relationships since we're all together and together separately as well. I miss my friends; I can't allow us to lose ourselves because of our relationships.

When I received the text from Ryan this morning asking that we all come over for a night of *The Office* and junk food, it's all I've been able to think about. Hadley and I arrived a half hour ago and have been too busy chatting to start the show. My stomach rumbled indicating that I hadn't fed myself today. Oops, lucky for me my friends are ready with snacks.

My chest tightens with the comfort and normalcy as the scent of freshly popped popcorn fills the room. Hadley skips like a schoolgirl with her first crush as she makes her way back to where Ryan and I are seated. She's got a large bowl overflowing with the delicious snack ready to share between the three of us while we curl up into a cuddle puddle on Ry's couch.

Michael Scott is causing so much chaos within the episodes that I'm usually giggling, but I can't focus enough on what's happening to react like I normally would. It's one of our favorite shows. The heaviness of what I'm hiding from my friends is starting to weigh on me the more time I'm with them. It's not until we're at the end of season two and Casino Night is on that I even realize just how quiet I've been.

"Pickle," Ryan pokes me in the ribs playfully as she sits up to lock her eyes onto mine. I blink rapidly when I realize she's speaking to me. "You, ok? You've been oddly quiet tonight. You love this episode."

My mind races as I think quickly while trying not to lie. A wicked grin splits my face as I respond. "I'm just tired. I've been getting pretty intense workouts lately."

"Oh, you are so getting nailed!" Ryan shrieks and lifts the remote in her hand, once she presses the button to stop the next episode from playing, she turns to me with anticipation.

"It's not like we hadn't been having sex before, it's just different now. It's more intense," my confession comes out with more confidence than I feel. "My vagina has never been so happy to have a night off," I giggle trying to make light of the subject.

Hadley shifts next to me before she chimes in with her own line of questioning. "Just how much sex are you having?"

"Uhm, well. A few times a day." I admit as my cheeks flush.

Suddenly a booming voice sounds, shocking all of us. "Do I need to step up my game?" Greyson, Ryan's boyfriend, is standing in the hallway with his bare chest on full display.

The three of us scream as Hadley grabs a throw pillow and takes the name literally because she pelts it with a force I've never seen her use, aiming directly at him. Her aim is true as the decorative pillow connects squarely in his face. The two of us cheer while Ryan stands and saunters over to him.

Hadley and I watch the two of them as they get lost in one another. The two of us smirk when they obviously forget that we're in the building until Hadley clears her throat. Watching the two of them together did more for me than I would ever admit to them. It also has me wanting to go home and enjoy the rest of my night with my partners.

I climb the stairs to the back door two at a time since Karma has been closed for several hours now. My overwhelming need to have Anya and Clay has my pussy clenching at the thought. Once I'm inside, I hear soft grunts which make my already needy cunt ready for what's to come.

With soft steps, I undress while I walk through the apartment to our bedroom. My clothes are strewn on the floor along the hallway. Clay's noises increase in volume the closer I get. Cautiously, I peek around the open door to see Anya on her knees servicing him. By the way his head is thrown back and the sensual sounds he's making, I can tell she's doing a damn good job.

She must sense me because her eyes pop open as soon as I enter the room. I continue my silent adventure, closing the distance to the dresser where my toys are. I pull out a bottle of lube and a toy I bought when Anya came back into my life. I didn't expect to have a chance to use it on Clay, much less fulfill his fantasy. Every bit of willpower is tested as I insert my side of the toy and make no noise in response to the fullness it provides. My feet carry me over to where Anya is still getting her face fucked by our man. I glide my fingers through her hair, distracting her from the task at hand.

"Fuck!" Clay groans in frustration as his eyes flutter open and he takes in the room finally spotting me. His eyes hooded with arousal brighten when he realizes I'm there. "Hey, Princess," the greeting is barely audible as he pants trying to catch his breath.

"Hey, baby," I greet him. "Why don't you let Anya catch her breath, I have something I want to do."

My excitement must show on my face because his brows furrow. When he glances down he sees that I've got the double-sided strap on already fully sheathed inside me and strapped for him.

"Oh fuck!" He whimpers.

"We're going to start on all fours and you're going to thank Anya for taking care of you like the good little slut she is for us." I instruct, praising the sex toy gods that we've been prepping for this since he told Anya about this fantasy. His eyes sparkle with anticipation.

Clay listens easily enough while Anya crawls onto the bed before he joins her. He crawls up her body and presses a soft kiss to her lips before turning awkwardly to kiss me. I give in to the kiss for a moment before helping him adjust on the bed a bit. I chuckle before forcing him down so that his ass is in the air and his face is mere inches from Anya's glistening cunt.

I pop open the bottle of lube, dripping a generous amount on the tight ring of muscle. Carefully prepping him, I slide one finger in slowly, massaging the inner walls of his perfectly sculpted ass. When he's used to it and angling for more, I slide in another until I'm eventually at a third and he's begging for more. I squirt more lube out, this time directly onto the toy, stroking the length to make sure it's good and ready for the way I want to nail our man. Once satisfied, I notch the tip at the tight hole and slide the head in.

"Fuck! Kat!" He growls out, a needy whimper following. I give him a moment to adjust before he quietly begs, "More, please."

It takes several gentle thrusts before the strap is fully seated inside his ass.

"Let me know when you're ready," I coax.

"Move, I need you!" The way he begs when he's at my mercy is one of the sexiest things I've ever experienced.

The moment he's comfortable, he lowers his face and buries himself between Anya's thighs. She lets out a breathy moan. She must have been so entranced by what I was doing to Clay she didn't realize he was ready for her.

I begin to pick up the pace, which only makes him groan and moan his appreciation into her pussy.

"Jesus Christ, I'm going to come!" She shouts into the spacious room.

I grin down at her and driver harder into Clay, my nails biting into his hips as I fuck him. "The sooner you do, the sooner he gets to fuck that pretty little mouth of yours, Bunny."

That reminder sends her over the edge. Her body shudders under him as she finds her release. He continues to lap at her sensitive clit for several moments before finally letting up.

"Princess," Clay's husky voice is still so needy.

"I'm going to pull out. And lay down. You're going to ride this dick and fuck her mouth simultaneously. Understand?" I instruct.

"Fuck, Kat, you being in charge is so fucking hot." Clay grips his cock and pumps from root to tip once, twice before he sees my glare and stops while he lets out a dark chuckle.

Once I'm laying on the bed, Clay mounts me like the good boy he is and cautiously sinks down on my strap. The way this purple silicone disappears inside his forbidden hole has my pussy throbbing around my own piece of silicone. I give him a few moments to get used to the position before I nod at Anya to join us.

"Fuck, Little Rabbit. I'm not going to last in this position." His confession lights a fire deep in my belly. As soon as Anya has her mouth latched around his cock I thrust my hips, getting the strap as deep as possible. "Fuckkkkk! Princess!" Clay roars.

"Yes, baby?" I feign innocence.

"If you do that again I'm going to blow my load down Anya's throat." He groans as he continues bouncing as he impales himself repeatedly.

"Bunny, get ready." I murmur and click the button on the remote I've had in my hand at the same time that I thrust my hips upward again to bury myself deeper inside him.

A slew of gibberish passes Clay's lips as he unleashes the release he's been needing on Anya. His hand palms the back of her head holding her in place where he keeps her still to make sure she swallows every last drop of his seed.

Chapter Twenty-Nine

Floral spandex stretches tightly over Kat's ass as she moves into downward dog. My cock swells at the sight and it takes everything in me not to react. That is until she transitions several more times with the rest of the class and they end up in a plow pose. Yes, I in fact have plowed her in that position, and it is glorious. An image of Anya in the same pose taking Kat's strap and me at the same time forms in my mind, time stands still as I compose myself. Fuck me, there's an item to add to my bucket list.

I shake the images out of my head and try to focus on the class as a whole. Kat stands tall when she notices a client not quite in the correct position. After taking a few minutes to help them correct the stance she makes her rounds eying everyone to ensure their safety.

"Don't you get enough of her now?" I turn to see Jenna and Tina, their amusement clear on their faces. Jenna, the one who spoke continues, "Especially now that she's living with you?"

"I'll never have enough of them." I confess, my lips twitch as the memory of last night flashes in my mind.

When I glance back to the girls Tina cocks a brow at me. Jenna's face scrunches with confusion. Shit, I shouldn't have mentioned Anya. Fuck. My brain whirls and I pull the first topic that I know will distract them. "Have you been practicing your wink?" I tease Tina.

She grins at me with a sly smirk, "You know what." She bounces on her toes with excitement. "I have been practicing."

Jenna grumbles something inaudible beside her. Immediately Tina attempts to wink at me, but her face still contorts into what looks like a seizure. Shaking my head I choke out a laugh.

"Hey guys!" Kat's sweet voice cuts through the conversation as she leans into me. "What's so funny?" She arches a brow as her gaze darts between the three of us.

"Your boyfriend insists on taunting my woman." Jenna snorts as she wraps her hand around Tina's slim waist and drags her off to begin their workout. Unable to stop the grin that stretches across my face as I watch them get settled on their machines.

"Princess, may I see you in my office?" The question comes out with no emotion, I'm proud I hold my anticipation in that she doesn't know what's coming.

"Uh, sure?" She takes the lead and adds a little bounce to her step as she saunters away from me. Fuck, she's a cock tease. Maybe she does know what I want.

I follow behind like a lost dog. Let's face it without her, and now Anya, in my life I would be a lost puppy. Once we're safe within the office walls, I close the door.

"What's up?" She asks as she spins on her heel to face me.

Before she has a chance to ask anything more, I close the distance between us and crash my mouth to hers. Our lips part in unison and I tease her tongue with mine. When I drag my tongue over her lips she takes the bait, sliding hers into my waiting mouth. I suck her into my mouth, one hand in her hair, holding her in place, the other gripping her ass as she grinds her hips against my thigh looking for release.

I pull back, separating from her and she whines. It's the sexiest sound I've ever heard.

"Why? What? What was that for?" She whimpers, her hands grip the hair at the nape of my neck sending even more blood straight to my groin.

"I may fall asleep with you and Anya in my arms, but baby I can never get enough of either of you. I'm just lucky enough to be able to take advantage of extra time with you while we're here." I wink at her and smack her ass playfully.

"Fuck, you owe me at least two orgasms for that." She pouts.

"Such a hard ask, but for you, I'll make it four." A wicked grin spreads across my face as a plan forms in my mind. "And then let Anya use the strap on you. She can use my release as a lube for both ends of the toy."

A soft whimper escapes Kat. The way her bright eyes glitter with desire has me grip my dick through my shorts. They'll be the death of me, and I am so here for it.

"Now?" She begs quietly.

"You still have clients, Babygirl." I press a soft kiss to her forehead and gesture for her to get back out onto the floor.

"You're the worst." She groans.

"I love you, too." I smirk.

Closing the door behind me, I start to walk in the direction Kat is headed only to crash into her back. My hands dart to her biceps to hold her in place and make sure she doesn't fall. "Son of a bitch." I groan, as my heart thuds violently in my chest, "are you ok?"

When I glance up and see where she's looking the blood drains from my face. Oh hell. Not again.

Chapter Thirty

Why? Why is she here? Of all people. Why? My blood runs cold, and I stop short, not realizing that Clay is right behind me. I feel his hard body pummel against my back, his strong hands grip my biceps which keeps me in place while he regains his footing.

"Son of a bitch, are you ok?" He sounds startled and confused as to why I stopped. He must not have noticed her yet.

It takes a few moments as I take in the slender woman before me. Her dark hair resembles my natural color though the short bob is the same style she's had since as far back as I can remember. She's still the petite woman with the eyes identical to mine. It's not until I take a step back and see the full image does everything from the day of the accident comes rushing back.

The dark SUV is aimed right for them, the two people I love most in this world. With blackout tinted windows I can't see who is driving. I dart across the street faster than I ever have before. The moment I reach them and tackle them to the grass I look up to see the brightest red glasses. I wonder if Sally Jessy Raphael is the one behind the wheel. Wait – isn't she like ninety? The three of us are rolling down the hill as tires screech in the distance.

"It was you!" I cry out the accusation. "You tried to kill them!"

My mother smirks at that and shrugs while pushing the same red glasses I remember up to sit on her face. Not admitting to anything.

"Since your father failed to obtain the information we asked for the last time he was here, I thought it was time I paid you a visit, Katrina." Her voice is as harsh and cruel as the last time I saw her. "Where is my daughter?"

My body goes rigid. It's the first time I've seen this woman in years. Seeing my father shocked me. It broke my heart all over again. But seeing this cunt before me – my vision blurs and everything before me is a thick fog of red. I snap, not broken, but absolutely enraged.

"You mean the one that you abandoned because you didn't like the fact that she eats pussy?" My inability to hold back the fury for not only myself but for my big sister is real. "Or the one that you forced to endure being used as some douchebag's sex slave for a year and didn't do a thing to stop it?"

An expression that one can only describe as abject horror appears as the blood drains from her face. She's shocked that I've called her out when I've never stood up for myself in the past with them. I never knew about everything that happened with Penny until recently, and even now, I feel like there's more my sister hasn't told me.

"How dare you!" My mother attempts to scold me. "You will not speak to me like that."

Clay's fingers tighten around my biceps as I try to lunge for her, and he clears his throat.

"Mrs. Kensington," his smooth whiskey voice sounds behind me.

"Don't speak to me! You're encouraging her repulsive behavior." She snarls at the man actively holding me back from laying into the woman before me.

Clay chuckles darkly as his arms wrap around me. "Ma'am, just as I told your husband, I don't give a flying fuck who you are. You will not speak to or about Kat in that manner."

My mother rolls her eyes and turns her attention back to me.

"Where is Penny?" She repeats her earlier question with more venom in her voice, forcing evenness into her tone that I know she doesn't feel. "As you know, we're aware she's been in contact with you. Where is she?"

"It doesn't matter where she is, you'll never find her." My response is filled with anxiety and comes out more shrill than I mean it to. "She's finally safe from you and your psychotic husband."

"She'll never be safe!" She retorts through gritted teeth.

"Not with you she won't be." With a shrug of my shoulders I continue, "now get the fuck out of here or we're calling the police."

My mother rolls her eyes at me and laughs maniacally as she turns to leave. She replies with a quick glance over her shoulder. "Next time, we won't miss."

I have no time to respond before she leaves the gym. My body is vibrating with anger, Clay steps away from me and curses under his breath.

"Your parents need a goddamn shock collar," he growls.

"They need something stronger than that." I fume, "I've got to call Auggie."

My feet have a mind of their own as they bolt for the office where I pull my phone from the desk drawer. I frantically tap the screen until I navigate to his contact and press the green call button. It rings once before he answers.

"Hey, KitKat." I can hear the smile in his voice.

"Aug - mom was just here." I pause to take a deep breath. "She's the one who tried to kill them. I recognized her glasses when she was here."

My brother's heavy breathing on the other side of the phone is the only reason I know the line is still open.

"She said..." I sob as the entire conversation plays back in my mind, "She said next time they won't miss. Auggie – I – I'm freaking out. They're still looking for Pen."

"Tell me exactly what she said to you." He demands.

And so, I spend the next few minutes going over the conversation. I could hear a chuckle come from my big brother when I shared how I called her out on everything. When I finish telling my story I wait for a response.

"I'm proud of you, Kat," he pauses and clears his throat. I hear Chloe and Echo talking in the background. "I love you, KitKat. I'll take care of this. All of it."

The line disconnects and he's gone without another word.

Chapter Thirty-One

Anya

My eyes focus on the list of walk-ins. Oh, the next person requested me. I wonder who referred them.

"Karston?" I call out into the waiting area, what a unique name.

An older gentleman with greying hair stands and strolls toward me. He looks extremely familiar; but I can't place him. I shrug it off and smile as I greet him.

"Hi! Welcome to Capelli Studio. My name is Anya, if you'll follow me right this way, we'll get started." I smile at the man and wave my hand in a gesture to follow me.

He's very quiet and doesn't respond to my greeting. We walk to my station in silence, I spin my dark chair to face him so he's able to take a seat.

"So, what are you looking to have done today?" I ask with a warm smile plastered across my face. It's my customer service smile.

"Short on the sides, a little longer on top." Karston grunts out.

"Alrighty!" I spin him to face the mirror and drape a dark cape over his front, clasping it around his neck to avoid any excess hair from getting onto his clothing.

I spend the next twenty minutes attempting to hold a conversation with the man, but he refuses to give in to my charm. This isn't exactly new, on occasion we get clients who request silent appointments, which I do love. Not having to have small talk, it's wonderful. But there is something about this man that has my anxiety increasing with every moment of silence that passes between us.

A sigh of relief breaks free when I finish, but before he stands the man stares at me through the mirror and speaks to me unprompted for the first time since I greeted him.

"How long have you been fucking my daughter this time?" He growls the question out so low no one else can hear him.

"I – what? Who are you?" I ask, fearing I already know the answer.

"How long have you been fucking Katrina? I know you left her once before; I thought you grew a conscience and realized how wrong you were to be doing what you were." He scoffs.

My gaze is locked on him through the mirror. Unable to find words, my mouth opens and closes again without a sound passing through.

"I thought my wife was a little over the top when she tried to eliminate both you and the boy." Karston snorts before continuing, "all things considered, I'm fine with him bedding my daughter even if Beatrice isn't."

His words slowly process, and I realize what he's just admitted to. Fury radiates through me as the pieces come together. *What in the actual fuck.*

"Get out!" I scream as tears begin to fall. I sense Axel's gaze at my outburst.

"Calm down, dear. This was just a friendly warning to stay away from my daughter, you dirty whore." He removes the cape himself and stands, dragging his gaze up and down my body like I'm something beneath him. "If you continue this abomination of a relationship with my daughter, we won't miss next time."

"Get the fuck out!" My voice cracks with how loud I shout this time.

Karston stands just as Axel approaches my side. The three of us are in silent a standoff for several minutes before Kat's father finally walks away. My blood boils, I fall back into Axe as everything sinks in. Her parents, the love of my life's parents, tried to kill us.

"Anya? What just happened?" Axel asks softly as he grips my bicep to turn me around to face him.

"I need to talk to Kat." I rush out and run to the back of the salon while digging my phone from my pocket. Once the device is in my hand, I send a message to Kat.

Anya:

I need you. ASAP. Your dad was just here.

Just as quickly as I press send my phone rings, with her picture on the screen. I swipe to answer and barely breathe out a greeting.

"Hey."

"What the fuck did he do?" She snarls through the phone.

Even though she's rightfully angry, the sound of her voice is a balm to my soul. My brain is working on overdrive to be able to respond with actual words and not screams or sobs. It takes me a moment, but when I can speak, I explain everything that happened. Everything he said to me.

"Bunny, don't move. I'm coming to get you." Her voice is unsteady as she speaks, her own anger cuts through her words.

"Yeah." I sigh and hang up just in time to look up and see Axe in front of me.

"What the fuck?" A worried expression is etched across his beautiful features.

"Kat's father." I admit as I frantically glance around the room. "Axe, they're coming to pick me up. I need to be with them right now." My hands shake as I tell my best friend I'm leaving for the day.

He nods cautiously and takes a seat next to me. I sob as his arm snakes around my shoulders and holds me tight to him. I feel Axe's body go stiff a moment before he speaks.

"I don't know all of the details, but if anything more happens to her." He snarls as I take in a terrified Kat

"Rick!" I shove him, "they didn't do this."

"Louis, this wouldn't be happening if it weren't for them." He stares at me with a pleading look.

Kat takes a step forward, the air around her sparks with the anger I can sense radiating off her.

"Axel, I appreciate that you have Anya's best interest at heart. I promise you, we do too." She holds her hand out to me which I take and stand next to her, our fingers laced together. "They won't get away with this."

"I'm coming with you." He announces.

"What about our clients?" I ask exasperated.

Axel is on his feet a moment later strolling as if he has no care in the world to the front of the salon.

"Lori can close and call everyone." I see his shoulders raise and fall as he shrugs. "I'll meet you there."

An hour later, I have a bag of clothes packed and we're in the car headed back to Karma. Kat dials a number while we are sitting in traffic. A voice I recognize speaks through the speakers.

"KitKat?" Augustus' voice is cautious as he speaks. "What happened?"

I see a lone tear fall down her cheek as she speaks.

"Dad was at Anya's salon and threatened her too." She explains.

"Son of a bitch." His growl reverberates through the vehicle.

"Auggie, I'm fucking terrified." She admits to her big brother.

"Give me a few days. We will handle it." He snarls and the call disconnects.

My face must show my confusion. I know her brother is protective, but what can he do? She squeezes my hand and leans in to press a soft kiss to my lips.

"If anyone can get our peace back, it's them." Her confession both calms me and worries me. What exactly are they going to do?

We walk up the steps to their apartment to find Clay and Axel sitting on the couch chatting while Anyanka Jenkins is on the television screen singing about bunnies.

I groan, "Why do I like either of you?" And storm off to the bedroom where I collapse onto the mattress.

Chapter Thirty-Two

O ne month later

My bright blue nails gleam in the light as Anya sits next to me with one hand sprawled on my thigh while I'm gingerly holding the other in my own. With a practiced stroke I apply her favorite pink glittery polish, 'cosmic something' by a popular nail polish company. Why she decided we needed to do each other's nails tonight is beyond me, but the way she's smiling in this moment is worth it. The sound of a football game fills the room as Clay sits behind me, his arm snug around my middle while I finish the first coat.

This past month has been nerve-wracking. My parents have been quiet and stayed away from us since I spoke with Auggie, but he stopped answering my calls after I told him about dad accosting Anya at her salon. We've stayed together as much as possible and Axel has been transporting her here every night after work. I know she likes her space, but being apart isn't an option I can get on board with until I know they're no longer a threat.

"Princess?" Clay hums in my ear. "Why are you so tense?"

I glance over my shoulder to see his eyes boring into me with concern. I lean into him even more and tilt my head back to give him access to my mouth. He takes the hint and kisses me softly. My lips twist into a relaxed smile.

"My brain is working on overdrive," I admit.

"Hmm," is his only response as my phone begins to buzz before he can say anything else.

Anya hands me the device from the coffee table in front of where we sit on the couch. I tap the green button to answer when I see Hadley's name on the screen.

"Hey babe! What's up?" I ask as Anya stiffens when I take the call. I know it's killing her not to meet them. I'm just not ready.

"Hey, Ry is on her way over here." Hadley takes a breath before rushing out, "she just dropped Greyson at the airport. She needs us."

"I'll be there as soon as I can." I reply and turn to Anya as I disconnect the call.

"Go. It's fine." She waves me off.

"Bunny, it won't be like this forever." I try to comfort her, which is pointless. She's pissed and she has every right to be. "I'm sorry."

I've been at Hadley's for twenty minutes sipping the most delicious wine I've tasted. Hadley paces the floor as she checks her watch again since I've been here.

"Babe?" I ask while my gaze follows her path across the room.

"She should have been here by now." Hadley says into her hand as she bites her nails. "Something's wrong."

"Don't panic, try calling her again." My voice calmer than I feel as the anxiety radiates from Had in waves.

"I've been calling her and it just rings." She sobs.

My mind refuses to go to the worst case scenario. I can't allow it because then that would mean we haven't protected her. Hadley and I would never forgive ourselves. She's fine. She has to be. I grab my phone from my pocket and try her number for myself. It rings through to voicemail. The same thing happens when I try again.

Fuck.

With an unsteady breath, I pull up the contact I have for Benny and press the call button. It only takes a moment before he answers.

"Detective Grant," he answers with his deep on-duty voice.

"Benny," I whisper his name, and swallow hard before continuing. "It's Kat."

"What's up?" Concern evident in his tone, he keeps the same cadence he had when he answered.

My heart begins to race as I explain what's happened. Or what we don't know for sure that's happened, but all things considered, we need to be careful.

"Ry was supposed to come to Hadley's after she left the airport. She should have been here an hour ago." A pause so pregnant occurs, I have to check my phone to make sure we're still connected before I continue. "Under normal circumstances we wouldn't reach out to you for her being late. But with the stalker still out there..."

"Don't move. I'll be there in ten." He snaps before disconnecting the call.

Hadley and I haven't left one another's side since we realized Ry was abducted. It's been days and now that Greyson is back, they finally have a lead. Or, Greyson and Connor have a lead. They haven't made it clear just that we need to be available when they find her. A harsh repetitive pounding in my chest has been keeping me from being able to relax. My anxiety is at an all-time high and I haven't been able to speak to Clay or Anya since I left, apart from a few text messages. Tears threaten when the phone rings again. Hadley answers at a record pace.

"Baby?" She sobs into the phone as I keep my arms tight around her shoulders. "Oh my god! Oh my god!" She says several times before she looks at me with a smile in her eyes. "We'll be there."

Hadley disconnects the call and stands; she reaches her hand out for me to take and follow her.

"Had, what's happening?" My voice cracks as I ask the question.

She grins while she pulls me up. "They found her, all I know is that she's alive. We need to get to the hospital."

As soon as we arrive, we rush to the ambulance bay, the same place that Ryan and I went with Hadley when we found her. I tear up at the memory while we wait and reach to hold Hadley's hand, grounding myself in this moment. A rig backs in and the doors open quickly. Greyson steps out along with an EMT who snaps at Hadley and I.

"You two can't be here," her high-pitched voice is like nails on a chalkboard.

"If you think I've been unbearable, try keeping these two away from her." Greyson grunts out which she rolls her eyes at but allows us to follow.

When we are finally led to her room, I'm able to take a look at our friend. She's broken and bruised. Wrapped in a blanket that looks like it's seen better days. From the way she refuses to let go of Greyson, I'm terrified I know what she's been through.

A doctor enters and tries to tell him to step away from Ryan when Hadley jumps in and hands the doc a new asshole. She has grown into such a fierce and outspoken woman with everything she's faced. My heart aches as I think back to when we were in this same hospital with her. And here we are, seemingly doing it all over again with Ryan now.

Chapter Thirty-Three

Anya

Three weeks later

I step through the doors of Alchemy Ink. It's been a long-time coming, considering when I moved here, one of the deciding factors was because of Dixie. What can I say, once you start getting tattoos, you just can't stop. They're like Pringles and pistachios and Friends episodes.

The man I saw at the bar not long after I had run into Katis standing behind the counter. My jaw drops in shock as he greets me.

"Anya?" His smile is so warm and welcoming, I feel at ease immediately.

"Hey! I didn't expect to see you here." I flash a bright smile at him. "How did everything turn out with," I don't finish when I see a woman that I recognize, only because I've seen her picture on Kat's social media.

Ryan.

I school my features to keep them from realizing anything may be wrong.

Greyson grins at her, "It's great. Ryan, this is Anya. Anya, Ryan."

"Do I know you?" Her voice is harsh, she looks like she is about to tear my head off.

"No?" Shit, I glance at Greyson and back to Ryan. "I have an appointment with Dixie."

As if she can tell that I'm in a panic, Dixie appears. The theme from *Saved by the Bell* starts playing in my head as soon as I see her which makes me chuckle.

"Hey, bestie! Come on back, I can't wait to work on this poly piece. It's going to be beautiful!" Dixie pops her head out from around the corner, and I follow her back to her room.

When we saw Kat's tattoo for the first time I was in awe that she would permanently mark herself for us the way she did. It only seems fair to do the same and show my dedication to them as well. While I may have initially agreed to this arrangement because of Kat, Clay has dug himself into my heart as well.

Dixie and I have been friends for a while. She used to work at a tattoo shop an hour away from my parents which is where we first met. This is the first tattoo she's done for me though and I'm glad it's her that is marking me. As soon as we enter her room she closes the door and motions for me to get comfortable.

"So, what's going on? How's the fam?" She sings-songs as she finishes her set up.

"My parents are fine, but I assume you're asking about Kat and Clay?" I tease her as I lower my pants and take a seat on her table. Thankfully, I just waxed a few days ago, so there won't be any stubble for Dixie to work around. She's tattooing me in the same spot where Kat has hers.

"Obviously. I need all of that info." She taunts, as she preps my skin for the stencil. "The last time I saw you, you were still pining for the woman, even though you hadn't seen her since you left college."

The stencil is placed, showing exactly what I had imagined. A pickle makes up the center of the heart, a simple single line outlines it, holding the two of us together. It's finished off with a final line that ends in the poly symbol. Tying the three of us into one beautiful unit.

"It's perfect! I can't wait. Let's do this!" I squeal.

"Sweet!" She giggles and presses her toe against the foot pedal for her tattoo machine.

I get lost in the process. Something about tattoos relaxes me. The constant vibration and the pricks of the needle send me into a peaceful Zen. I start to doze when I hear Dixie speak.

"So how is everything with your partners?" She asks as she wipes away excess ink.

My lips turn into a grin, and I spend the rest of the appointment telling her everything I can think of about Kat and Clay. None of the dirty stuff, since I'm pretty sure Kat would lose her mind If she knew I shared our intimate details. By the time I've disclosed all of the details of my relationship, she's done. It's only taken two hours which is impressive since she hasn't been tattooing as long as my last artist. I stand and glance in the mirror to take in her artwork. The coloring of the pickle is a vibrant green while the wire is a rose gold.

"Dix, this is incredible! I can't wait to show them what you created!" Tears well in my eyes and I grip my chest as my heart soars.

Chapter Thirty-Four

A few weeks later.

My plan was to tell Hadley after Ryan and Greyson had ex-changed vows. I was going to pull her aside to share about Anya. I'm so tired of lying, and when Hadley asked me why Clay wasn't here, I had to tell her that someone called out at Karma. In reality, he and Anya are spending the evening together. Then Connor had to go and propose with her favorite freaking books. And to top it all off, Sara freaking Hurst was involved in the proposal. That damn Irishman.

Alannah knew what my plan was and has been sending me glances of encouragement all evening, but now that Hadley and Connor are standing before us, exchanging their own vows, it's hard to follow through. As I watch them give promises to each other about sickness and health and blah, blah, blah, I can't bring myself to insert myself into their wedding day and potentially bring down a day that I want her to be able to enjoy and remember fondly.

The two happy couples are swaying back and forth on a make-shift dance floor on the patio when I slink back into the house and meander toward the bathroom. When I step inside the oversized space, especially for a restroom, I breathe a sigh of relief. Tears flow down my cheeks, I am exhausted. A soft tap – tap – tap sounds against the door before a familiar voice speaks.

"Kat, love? It's Alannah, may I come in?" There's a mixture of joy and sadness in her tone.

I reach out and unlock the door, the doorknob twists and she enters cautiously immediately after. We stood in silence for a few moments. Alannah's warm stare follows me no matter what I do or where I pace in the large space.

"Kat, you know I love you, yeah?" She says as she gingerly takes my hand and leads me to the toilet and gestures for me to take a seat. She doesn't speak again until I respond.

"I know, I love you too, Lan." I reply as I sniffle back tears.

"Wonderful, now stop being a feckin' eejit and tell them." She scolds me like only a mother can. "They're right outside. I know you're in here talking yourself out of telling any of them. Do you think Anya or Clay deserve to be hidden like this?" She asks.

"That's not fair! I'm not hiding Clay, and you know why –" I try to explain but she cuts me off before I can finish.

"Don't give me that story. You know what I mean." She throws her hands in the air, obviously frustrated with me. "By not telling them about her, you're hiding him away, because they would both be here with you right now. Hadley only cares that you're happy!"

After glaring back and forth at one another for several minutes I finally reply through my anxious tears. "I know you're right, but what if she hates me because of Andy?" I sob. "I'm terrified I'm going to lose my best friend because I'm in love with them both."

Alannah kneels down before me and takes my hands in hers. She sits with me for a while, it could be minutes or hours. When she finally speaks, I feel a weight lift off my chest.

"Kat, she is your best friend. She will always support you." Lan squeezes my hands, "But the longer you lie to her about your situation, that is what will cause her to be upset with you."

She gives me another moment before she pulls me to my feet. She wraps her arms around my trim frame and squeezes me to her before releasing me.

"Do you really think she'll be ok with Anya?" I ask, my hands trembling as I reach for the door.

My body freezes in place and my eyes go wide when the door opens to expose Hadley with tears in her eyes. Shit.

"Had," I try to speak. To explain what she heard.

"Kat." She snarls at me. An attitude I've never experienced from my kind, sweet friend.

"Hadley, listen, I'm not sure how much you heard, but I need to explain." My voice shakes as I speak.

"No, get out." She growls as she dramatically gestures her manicured hand toward the front door. "Leave, right now."

"Please. Let me explain!" I sob and try to reach for her.

Hadley has never flinched away from me, until right now. My heart clenches in my chest as the history of our friendship flashes before my eyes. I lower my head in shame and step around her.

"I'm sorry Hadley. I love you." I choke back a sob, before rushing out the front door.

I sit in my car for a while, just waiting. I'm not sure if I hope one or both of them will come after me. I wish she would allow me to explain. I knew this would happen after what went down with Andy. It may be a different situation, and our story may be vastly different from hers, but it's upset her. Unable to wait any longer, I start my car and drive off toward home. Towards Clay and Anya.

At least it's out there now, no more hiding. It's odd, I feel a sense of relief and the heaviest pain I've felt in my life. It's worse than losing Anya all those years ago. My fear that I'm losing my best friends has my heart shredded into pieces. Will we be able to survive this?

Chapter Thirty-Five

Anya

The mouthwatering aroma of coffee overwhelms my senses as I step through the door of Mud House. It's not my first time here but it is my first time meeting Kat here. Quickly glancing around the space I spot her easily at the counter chatting with a beautiful redhead. I cautiously close the distance and step up behind her.

"Hey, Pickle." I say quietly.

She turns with a genuine smile, which I haven't seen in a few days since the wedding. She pulls me in for a hug and pecks my lips with a quick kiss. I go still, unsure how to respond. We hadn't discussed being fully public, and I hadn't thought she was ready, even if her friends knew.

"Hey, Bunny." She tangles my fingers with hers and turns to the woman behind the counter. "Kay, this is my girlfriend Anya, Anya, this is Kayleigh. She owns the Mud House."

Kayleigh extends her hand to me, which I take gingerly, still unsure of how I feel about any of this.

"It's wonderful to meet you!" Her warm smile makes me feel more welcome than I anticipated with any of Kat's friends, given Hadley's history.

"We'll see you later, Kay. Thank you for this!" Kat beams as she holds up two cups. One frozen drink and one hot.

Her warm hand lands on the small of my back as she guides me toward a table in the back of the café. I lower myself into an oversized burgundy armchair as Kat takes a seat across from me. Carefully, I lift the cup to my lips and blindly take a sip. The moment the hot liquid hits my tongue, I softly moan. It's the most delicious caramel mocha latte to ever pass my lips.

"Holy shit. This is amazing." I say a little louder than necessary.

Kat giggles and winks at me.

"I'm sorry I've been so moody the past few days." She says softly and takes my hand across the table, squeezing tightly. "I'm working through it, and I'm done hiding."

My heart thuds in a staccato rhythm as her words settle in. She's done hiding, she wants to be out. I glance up at her with tears welling in my eyes.

"Have you told Clay?" I ask as I lift the cup to my mouth, pulling in another sip of my delicious drink.

"This morning." Kat confesses before explaining, "I didn't want to wait to tell you and it didn't feel right to tell you over text."

Admittedly I don't register much else of our conversations after that confession. When she stands up and kisses me again my mind checks back in, realizing her break is over and I need to return to the studio.

"I'll see you at home?" She asks, a hopefulness in her voice.

"I'll see you tonight," I promise and stand, pulling her in for another kiss. "Thank you." I whisper when we separate.

My cheeks hurt from the smile splitting across my face as I enter Capelli. Axel and Lori are both with clients as I approach. His eyes dart to mine as I pass by and his brow arches in question. I shoot a wink at him before I disappear into the break room to drop off my purse.

The bell sounds that someone else has entered the salon. So, I carry my cup of heavenly coffee back to the front where I see a woman waiting at the front desk. I've never met her, but I've seen many pictures of her while catching up on Kat's social media life now that we're back together. I swallow hard, unsure if she knows who I am, and transition myself into customer service mode.

"Hi, welcome to Capelli studio. Do you have an appointment?" I ask as cheerfully as I can even though I know damn well she doesn't have an appointment.

"Hello," She smiles at me. "I don't, but I'd like to get my hair trimmed."

"Sure, follow me." I reply warmly.

Hadley is on my heels until she takes a seat at my station. I place my hands on my hips to hide the trembling.

"What would you like to get done today, babe?" I ask.

It only takes me ten minutes to trim the inch off that she requested, but when I'm done she stares at me through the mirror.

"Anya," she says my name while her eyes are locked on mine.

I feel the blood drain from my face, knowing damn well I didn't tell her my name hoping to avoid a confrontation. Shit. God damnit.

"Alannah told me where you work." She confesses, "I wanted to meet you before I go see Kat."

"Okay." I drag out the word confused by what her plan is.

"I understand why she didn't tell me, but that is something I'll discuss with her. The reason I'm here, besides Ryan – Kat is my best friend. Clay may have been the one to get her through the initial loss of you, however we've been at her side helping to build her back up since the day we met her." Her eyes shine with emotion, "as long as you will cherish her this time and you're not going to leave when things get hard, you have my support."

"I – I – thank you, Hadley." I stutter my response.

She nods and stands, placing her hand in mine.

"Holy shit, you're stunning." I hear a voice behind me and groan.

Hadley laughs as Axel approaches us. He nudges my arm with his elbow silently asking for an introduction.

"Absolutely not. This is one of Kat's best friends and she's married." I scold him, only making Hadley laugh even harder. "I may not have met her husband, but I've heard enough about the man to know only a mature Henry Cavil, so long as he can pull off an Irish accent, would drag her attention from him. Even then, from what Kat says, it's unlikely."

Axel's eyes go wide as he glances between Hadley and myself, for the first time in our friendship the man is speechless.

"Oh my god, you're going to fit right in." Hadley snorts from behind me. When I turn to face her, she pulls me in for a hug. "We'll all get together soon so we can get to know you." She smirks before waving goodbye and disappearing out of the studio.

"What in the actual fuck, Anya! When the fuck did that happen?" Axel whisper-shouts at me.

"Well, I was off the last two days and didn't get a chance to tell you." I shrug. "It came out at the wedding this weekend and well, I guess that was her way of checking up on me to make sure I'm good enough for her friend."

Axe shakes his head in shock and drags me back to the break room to get the rest of the tea he missed out on while we've been working today.

Chapter Thirty-Six

"Come on babe, you can do another set." The encouragement rolls off my tongue so easily. Tina presses with everything she has into the free-weights to give me the last set I asked for. "Great job!" I croon.

"I really fucking hate you today." Tina growls as she wipes the sweat from her face with a small hand towel she carries with her.

No matter how many times she tells me this, she comes back to me again and again. If this were any other type of relationship I would be concerned about toxicity, however, she literally pays me to do this to her on a weekly basis.

"Love you too, babe," I grin flirtatiously at her and wink.

"I'm telling the wife you're being mean again." She laughs and sticks her tongue out before walking away.

My wide smile fades as soon as I turn toward the door to see Hadley standing at the front counter. My surroundings blur, focused only on my friend, unsure where we stand. She waves awkwardly in greeting; I nod my head in the direction of the office so we can have some privacy. When we enter the office Clay is at the computer, yet again, he glances up from the screen smiling when he sees me until Hadley appears.

"Hey, Hadley." He offers a weak greeting as we walk past to the apartment entrance.

As soon as we enter the apartment, I gesture for her to take a seat on the couch across from me. Once I make myself comfortable, I keep my gaze trained on her and wait for her to say her piece.

"Kat," Hadley starts. "Babe, I love you so much."

Tears sting at the corner of my eyes as she watches me.

"I know, I love you too." I confess, "you are one of my best friends."

As soon as I finish my response, she's on her feet pacing the floor in front of me. It takes a few minutes of no other words being spoken between us when she finally breaks the silence again.

"Listen, my reaction has nothing to do with you being with both of them." She laughs to herself. "Honestly, I like Anya, I think she's good for you."

"Wait, what?" Her words make no sense in my already chaotic thoughts.

Hadley is still pacing, as she wears a divot into the floor.

"I am upset that you hid it from me. You didn't give me a chance to hear it from you." She's waving her hands around, unable to keep any part of her body still while she expresses her emotions. "Andy's actions have nothing to do with how I feel about people who have multiple partners. You deserve so much love, and you've refused to allow yourself that for so long. I'm happy for you."

The whoosh – whoosh, whoosh – whoosh, of my pulse thuds so loud in my ears as I take in what she's saying. My body trembles with such overwhelming emotion it shocks me when Hadley rushes over to me, her arms wrap tightly around my shoulders.

"You're happy for me? Really?" I ask through a shaky breath.

"Babe, I'm thrilled for you." She replies quietly into my ear. "I just needed some time to digest. I understand why you didn't tell me. It just took a minute for me to process."

I pull away to grab a tissue from the side table to wipe away the tears that are falling free from my eyes. My heart stutters when I realize we will be ok.

"Can we rewind though; what do you mean you think she's good for me? How do you know?" I ask, unable to shake the earlier comment.

"I may have gotten her info from Alannah and tracked her down this morning," Hadley shrugs.

"You? Why?" I'm unable to complete a sentence because her words aren't making sense.

"We needed to make sure she wasn't going to break your heart again. Speaking of 'we,' I made Ryan sit in the car all morning. Can she come up?" Hadley rushes out.

"What? Yes, of course. Oh my god. What did you say?" I ask, my mind reeling from this new information.

Hadley digs her phone out of her purse and taps the screen a handful of times before she sets it back down to continue our conversation.

"I just made sure she understood that we wouldn't tolerate her not being here for the right reasons. Then she told her friend to back off me and compared Connor to a mature Irish Henry Cavill." She giggles as she explains. "I like her."

"And I'm pissed because I saw her at Alchemy, and it didn't click who she was when I heard her name." I hear Ryan groan as she steps into the apartment. "She's hot though, so I get it."

Hadley and I exchange an amused glance before we burst out laughing. I shake my head thrilled to have my friends here and able to share everything with them. Ryan takes a seat on the couch with us where they spend the next hour rapidly firing questions at me about Anya and how she came back into the picture.

"Kat." I hear Clay's somber voice from the stairway.

When I turn to look at him two uniform police officers are flanking him on either side.

"What's wrong?" I shout the question. My brief joy of reconnecting with my friends is gone.

"Hi, Miss Kensington?" The younger officer asks, I assume to confirm my identity.

"Yes, I'm Kat." I rush out. "What is it? What happened? Anya?" my heart pounds like a jackhammer in my chest. Every worst case scenario runs through my mind.

"Ma'am, I'm sorry to be the one to inform you, your parents have passed away." The same officer states, his tone matter-of-fact.

I hear a shocked gasp from the girls. Meanwhile, a wave of relief rushes over me when I know my girl is ok.

"What happened?" I hear myself ask.

They quickly explain that it was a house fire in the middle of the night and they didn't make it out. My mind whirls with what this means. And I'm a little shocked at the lack of grief that I feel at this news.

This past week has been a roller coaster, whirlwind, and clusterfuck of chaos and emotions. My parents are gone. Two people who have made my siblings and my lives hell for as far back as I can remember are finally gone from this world. Does it make me a terrible person for being so happy that they'll no longer be able to haunt my life?

Hadley and Ryan have been pushing me to meet with Amy which is why I am sitting in this waiting room staring at a wall with a poster I would have never expected to see in a therapist's office. It's a stunning floral print with pink wording *Do Epic Shit*. I can't help but smile when I read the words.

"Katrina Kensington?" I glance toward the familiar voice to see Amy. Still rocking the same pixie cut from when I first met her. She's been a huge part of my friend's healing journey, so I've met her a handful of times since Hadley first started working with her. She was even with us when we took Hadley to revisit her house after being released from the hospital.

"Amy, it's Kat." I wave my hand at her as I stand to follow into her room.

"I thought I recognized your name. How are you, sweetie?" She asks as I take a seat on her beige oversized couch.

Well, that's a loaded question. I spend the next hour explaining what's happened. Everything, from Anya's infamous return to my life, hiding it from my friends, Penny's return and subsequent disappearance followed by my parent's death. By the time I've finished word vomiting on her, she looks like she's been hit by a tornado.

"How in the actual fuck are you still functioning in everyday life after all of that?" She asks, her lack of filter is my absolute favorite thing about her. I understand why Hadley and Ryan still see her.

I shrug my shoulders and bark out a laugh. "Honestly, I have no clue."

We go over our time by twenty minutes so that I can answer her rapid-fire questions. I probably shouldn't find her concern as comical as I do. When we finish, I'm set with weekly appointments for the next six months. If I'm honest, a weight feels like it's been lifted off my shoulders as I step out of her office. The stress over all of this has been harder than I've let on.

For the first time in a while, my smile reaches my eyes without having to force it. I can breathe a bit easier now. I take my time making my way to my car. As soon as I'm inside, I pull out my phone and pull up my messages. I've been contemplating what to send. How to acknowledge it, but there is really only one thing I can say. I scroll through my contacts until I finally find the one I want and type out the words I want to say. The response bounces back quickly.

Kat:

Thank you.

Auggie:

Anything for you, KitKat.

Chapter Thirty-Eight

A year later

My knees press against the tiles of the shower as water droplets run down my face, Clay's fingers wrapped tightly around my wet hair. I hollow my cheeks as I suck him in deeper, Anya's fingers delve between my pussy lips and thrust inside me just as Clay juts his hips, so that his cock hits the back of my throat. I moan around his beautiful dick, my nails bite into the skin of his hips as I try to hold him in place.

He chuckles darkly and pulls out as An finds my G-spot. Her nimble fingers massage the sensitive spot inside me while she takes Clay into her mouth. My eyes roll back as I reach the edge, which only intensifies the moment. I hear Clay's guttural moan as he finds his own release, emptying himself into her waiting mouth. I cry out both of their names as my orgasm hits like a tsunami.

Before I can catch my breath, Anya's mouth crashes against mine. My lips part and our tongues immediately tangle around one another as we share Clay's release.

Anya whimpers into my mouth as my hands trail down her body. She's been squirming beside me on the verge of exploding this entire time. I thrust my tongue into her mouth, deepening the kiss at the same time that my fingers dive deep inside her. She moans into the kiss as I find the sensitive spot deep inside her, massaging in a way that makes her crazy. My other hand grazes her clit once, twice, before I pinch hard. Anya pulls away as her body convulses and she screams out, an intense orgasm flows through her. A proud grin spreads across my face when I feel a gush of wet heat flow between her legs down my hand.

"Jesus Christ." I hear Clay say from behind me. "You can get her to squirt? Why haven't we done this before?"

I giggle at his reaction. "Because it's my party trick. I only do it on special occasions." I wink over my shoulder at him. "Speaking of parties, we're going to be late."

I lean in and press a kiss against Anya's luscious lips before I climb to my feet.

My fingers are laced with Clay's, who follows behind me, my other hand holding Anya's as I trail behind her. The three of us make a train of sorts as we follow the hostess to where the baby shower is being held. The way the pink dress hugs her ass has heat rushing to my core. Before I can make an inappropriate comment to either of them, I hear Hadley squeal Anya's name in greeting as soon as she walks into the large open space. They're hosting the shower at Vissagio's restaurant. Inside the same private dining room that Hadley and Connor had their first date.

As worried as I had been about my friends accepting our relationship, it warms my heart when I see them together. Both Ryan and Hadley have taken Anya in without a second thought and include her in everything we do now.

"You are late!" Hadley pouts as she pulls us each in for a hug. She looks adorable in a pale pink floral pattern dress, her not-so-little bump making itself known.

"Sorry, Momma. I kept them distracted." Anya winks at her.

Connor steps up behind Hadley, his arms snake around her middle resting on her very swollen stomach. She's only seven months along, but with it being twins, the doctors anticipate her going on bed rest soon and likely an early labor.

"Who won?" Connors thick Brogue cuts through the chatter around us.

My eyes dart between An and Clay as I furrow my brow. *Won what?*

"Ryan called it. Sorry, Baby." She giggles as she turns to kiss her husband.

As if she could sense her name being brought up, Ryan walks over with her three-month-old son, Jess, in her arms. The brightest grin spreads across her face as soon as she sees us.

"Did I call it, or did I call it?" Ryan asks, a wicked glint in her eye as she waits for a response.

Clay clears his throat and asks, "What are y'all talking about?"

Greyson walks over with a handful of cash and hands it over to Ryan while shaking his head.

"Give me my boy, Kitten." He chuckles as he takes Jess from her arms.

Ryan giggles and claps her hands like a giddy school-girl.

"We made a bet on who would be the cause of your tardiness." She explains, "since you've told us about the three of you, you're never on time. We figured we would have some fun with it." She winks at Anya, "Thanks babe, first drink is on me next time we go to Finley's"

My cheeks heat with embarrassment.

"You did not!" I shout as I try to restrain my laughter.

It doesn't work, every single one of my friends and their partners are laughing with us. With a shake of my head I walk away to find Alannah leaving Clay and Anya with the others. She's off in a corner staring at her phone, her eyes glossy with unshed tears.

"Hey babe! What's going on?" I rush to sit down next to her, holding her hands in mine. She's facing away from the rest of the party goers, even her brother hasn't seemed to notice her clear emotional state.

"I'm fine, or I will be. It's Hadley and Connor's day. We'll chat later, love." She wipes the moisture from her eyes and flashes me a weak smile.

We sit in silence for a few minutes while she gets her emotions under control. As soon as she's able to breathe evenly she stands, dragging me along behind her. As we approach the rest of our friends and family, we see Jim and his wife Sabrina walk in with several large boxes.

"How are our favorite grandparents?" Connor asks the couple.

Jim is the valet from a restaurant that Hadley used to go to for a weekly dinner with her then husband. He has been more of a father to her then her own father had been over the years. And with Ryan and my parents being gone, the three of us have sort of adopted him and his wife. We started going to the restaurant with her last yar so that she had an excuse to still see him.

Alannah and I stand off to the side where we watch the exchange happen. Jim takes Ryan's son from Greyson while Sabrina embraces everyone individually. They've become an integral part of our little family.

After a while, we all settle in and have lunch and chat. I'm sandwiched between the two loves of my life while friends, colleagues and more of our little found family are here to celebrate Hadley and Connor's two little ones. Kayleigh and Liam's family are the last to show as Kayleigh made the cake. Something about - they didn't want anyone to sneak into the kitchen to see it before Hadley and Connor were ready for the announcement.

My lips twitch into a proud grin as soon as I see Hadley standing with Connor on her heels. The two of them are perfect for one another. I lean into Clay and pull An back into me as we wait for the two of them to speak. Connor clears his throat which brings all of the other conversations to an instant halt.

"Everyone, thank you for coming. My beautiful wife and I have been arguing profusely over names for our little ones." He chuckles as he pulls Had tightly into his side and presses a kiss to her temple. "It's important to both of us that the names we choose have special meaning." Connor explains.

"As you know, we're having twins." As soon as she says it, Kayleigh comes out with a huge cake covered in pink icing with the letters J and S on the side.

The room erupts in applause, hoots and hollers. I see Alannah start to cry as she smiles at her big brother and Hadley. Connor grins and waves his hands gesturing for us to quiet down.

"Some of you may know that in my previous marriage there was one man who was a constant in my life and stuck by my side throughout the good and bad. He is someone who made my every week just a bit brighter." She explains as she begins to tear up while she has her eyes locked on Jim as she motions for him to join them at the front of the room. When Jim joins them, she loops her arm around his and continues. "Jim, you have been such a wonderful part of my life over the past decade, even in the darkest of times and it would mean the world to me if we could name one of our daughters James, after you."

There isn't a dry eye in the place once she makes her announcement of the first name. He wraps her in a tight hug while he smiles and nods at her. He turns to shake Connor's hand before he turns to sit back with his wife, who has tears still streaming down her cheeks with a proud smile on her face.

"And for the second little one, since Sara Hurst was a huge part of our engagement." She smirks up at Connor with hearts in her eyes. "We will be naming our second daughter Sorcha."

Epilogue

Axel:

It's set

I grin down at my phone and inconspicuously show the screen to Clay while Anya is chatting away with our friends. He leans in and nips on my neck before he whispers in my ear.

"Let's get out of here so we can both be buried in her." I nod in response.

My sweet, extroverted Bunny takes her time to say goodbye to our friends. Meanwhile, I can hug my three girls and then run out. Not Anya, she has to make sure she says her farewells to everyone.

"Rabbit." Clay groans with impatience. She freezes, knowing that any time the *Little* isn't included she's in trouble. I chuckle as I see her excuse herself.

"Magic Mike, I didn't want to be rude." She sticks her tongue out at him and slaps his ass as she sways her hips with an extra bounce in her step while walking away.

"I call dibs on her ass tonight." I wink back at him as I follow behind her.

I rush up the stairs first to unlock the door while Clay and Anya take their time to catch up. My shoulders are pressed against the door as I watch the two of them close the distance between us.

"What are you doing?" Anya asks, which just makes me smile.

My hand grips the knob, and I twist my wrist before opening to expose our space, every hard surface covered in candles. Anya enters and glances around the space, her eyes filled with wonder.

"What the?" She asks as Clay and I follow closely behind her.

Anya has been spending most nights with us since my father accosted her at her place of work. My parents have been gone for almost as long, but it felt right to have her here, and she didn't object to it either. She hasn't officially moved in. Clay and I have been discussing it more and more lately. It doesn't feel right when she's not here. Whether it's in our space or in our bed. She is ours.

"A little over a year ago, I had invited you over here the same night I had planned on asking Kat to move in with me." Clay starts as he takes my hand, pulling me into his side. "Now, this is us asking you to make this our home."

Instead of speaking she rushes toward us and tackles us to the ground. Her lips crash against mine before she pulls away to kiss Clay. I'm giggling by the time she allows us to sit up.

"Yes, of course,yes!" She cries, "but how the hell did you do this?"

"Ahh, Louis. You're not the only one with a beautiful friendship." I reply, my tone light with amusement.

E ight years ago

The call came in a month ago. My husband abandoned us, through no fault of his own. He was run off the road by a drunk driver and was killed instantly. At least, that's what they told us. It's what I told my family when I asked my big brother to uproot his life and come help me raise my son.

Connor has been a chronic bachelor since college. His girlfriend left him to be with his best friend after he received some sort of inheritance. He's sworn off women since then. Alright, not women, relationships. He's a ride, a fine thing and can have a fling with anyone but he's refused to allow anyone close since she left. Which is why I knew he would keep the promise he made to me all those years ago. That he'd be here for me, no questions asked.

As I pull into my driveway I notice a dark SUV parked across the street. Odd, I've never seen it before and that spot was most definitely empty when I left to take Sean to school. I let out a defeated sigh as I unhook my seatbelt and reach for the door handle.

A dark figure is suddenly there, opening the car and hovering over me. My eyes go wide with fear, the stranger holds a finger over his lips to stay silent and forces me out. He manhandles me until we are inside. I turn on my heel ready to scream, realizing allowing him to get me inside was an idiotic move.

"Who the hell are you?" I shout at the man.

"Someone you're going to need to listen to." He grins at me with a darkness in his expression that has me schooling my emotions.

"What do you want?" I ask more calmly than I feel.

"Your husband wasn't killed by a drunk driver." He announces with so much conviction I can't help but believe him. "We cut his breaks, considering he kept trying to slip past his responsibilities. The thing is he owes my boss some money. Even in death he knew the deal. He still owes us a hundred thousand dollars."

"I'm sorry, what?" I ask exasperated.

"Sweetheart, he was in way deeper with a bookie than you can imagine." The man shrugs, "we'll give you a few weeks to pay up."

"You can't be serious!" I exclaim at the man as he retreats to my front door. There is no way he could expect me to have that kind of money in that short of a time. No freaking way.

"You'll figure it out, you don't want to risk Sean's only other living parent, do you?" He winks and slinks back out into the world.

For feck sake!

My heart races as I pull my top back on. The handsome man, Trager, who is seated before me has a devious smirk on his face but I'm not sure which way he's leaning.

It's been a week since the stranger came to me with the information that I have to pay for Colin's mistakes. My inability to ask for help has landed me in my current predicament. As I stand in front of my hopeful boss I take in my surroundings. It's nice, classy. Not what I would expect from what I've seen in movies.

"Listen Baby, you're gorgeous but if you want to step on my stage you're going to have to get a Brazilian." He chuckles as he drags his fingers through his short beard. "My customers don't do bush."

"You mean, if I get waxed I have the job?" I ask, barely able to hear my own voice over the pounding of my heart.

"Yea, you have a nice body and you can dance." He shrugs, "stop by to show me once you're bare and I'll get your stage name to put you on the roster."

"Oh lord, Jaysus, thank you so much! I will find a place right now." My eyes sting as they fill with unshed tears. "Thank you Mr. Trager, so much."

He waves his hand motioning for me to leave. Once my purse is secure on my shoulder I rush out of The Vault, the strip club I will be dancing at. Feckin hell, what has my life turned into.

I quickly move to my car and get in. Once the car is on, I turn on the heat and toss my head against the back of the seat and let out a strangled cry to let out my frustration and anxiety before I continue with the mission at hand. After a quick internet search while I sit in my car reading a handful of reviews I call Slick by Sidney for an appointment. Luckily for me, she has an open appointment in an hour.

Her studio is precious, set in a small cottage-like building just out of the city. It's painted a beautiful evergreen color. The quaint space is welcoming from the sign over the door to the plants that fill the open space once inside.

"Hi! Are you Alannah?" A girl barely out of high school sits behind the registration desk greets me as soon as I walk inside.

Oh shite.

"Hi, yes I am." I admit cautiously, anxiety bubbles in my chest, this girl can't have the education to do this as young as she looks.

"Hi! I'm Jess, Sid will be right with you." She smiles warmly at me.

Thank the lord.

A few moments pass when a young woman appears from a closed door at the far end of the waiting area. Her dark hair is pulled into a tight ponytail keeping her face free. She grins at me with a knowing gleam in her eye.

"Hi, Alannah, I'm Sidney. Let's get you taken care of, yea?" She calls and holds the door for me. "We'll be right through here."

I stand and close the distance between us as I follow her into the room where a long table is set up. A chair is set to the side to place your clothes. At least, that's what I assume it's there for. I swallow hard before I look at her again.

"This is your first time, right?" She asks with an amused expression.

"Is it that obvious?" I groan.

"Kind of. Usually I don't have to tell people to get undressed if they've done this before." She chuckles.

"Oh god, sorry." I rush and quickly undress. As soon as the clothes are on the chair I lay on the table and wait.

She makes the process simple, or she makes it seem like it's going to be simple. The application of the wax itself isn't bad. It's actually quite soothing. With a quick warning and an abrupt rip of the purple substance my soul is torn from my body.

"FECKIN' HOLY SHITE!" I shout as tears prick at my eyes yet again.

She giggles again. obviously enjoying the pain she's causing me.

"You're kind of evil, you know that?" I ask with a frustrated sigh.

"Hey, you called *me* babe, so what made you decide to do this?" She asks as she yanks the next piece which has me biting my fist.

"Long story short, I need quick money and got a job at The Vault. But the stipulation was I needed to be bare." I shrug as she continues.

"Oh, yeah, a few of my clients work there. Don't worry, you're in good hands." She snorts and pulls another strip of wax.

The next day, Trager gives me an ok to start, and as I approach the stage that night my heart begins to pound deep in my chest.

Here goes.

Acknowledgements

My family, your support during this journey has been incredible.

Tiesha – My PA. Lady, I don't know what I would do if you hadn't come into my life. Thank you for all of your hard work and helping me organize my chaos.

My alpha team, you are the MVP and I can't imagine this journey without you.

Sara - My boo. I'll forever be thankful that you slid into my DM's. You are phenomenal, and I love you!

K.D. - My ride or die, I love you and I'm so freaking proud of you!

To the FBI Agent, I hope this one kept you on your toes more than the last one.

Lastly, but most definitely not least, to every single one of you who has reached this page. There will never be enough words for me to express my love for you adequately. Thank you for reading this book. I cannot wait to share additional stories with you!

About the Author

I'm an introvert. Well, until you get to know me. Then I won't shut up. I'm married to my favorite PITA; he's the doctor to my Clara.

(IYKYK). We have a little boy who is growing way too fast and is already way too smart for my own sanity. I've had an unhealthy obsession with *Gilmore Girls* and *Buffy the Vampire Slayer* for years. You'll see the references throughout my writing. I've loved reading for as long as I can remember, but physical books with traditional novel paper give me the ick! So, you'll find me reading on my Kindle or listening to audiobooks on the regular.

Be sure to stalk me on all of my socials here